Oh, how she wanted this man.

He was a near stranger, yet she was a stranger to herself, as well. Her life, all she knew, all she felt, was narrowed down to when she'd opened her eyes in the woods and seen Ben.

"No past," he said, close to Megan's lips. "No future. Just now."

"Yes," she whispered. "Just now. I want you so much, Ben."

"Ah, Megan, I want you, too, but…" He shook his head. "No, this is wrong. You have a life beyond this moment. I can't—won't—take advantage of you. I'm so afraid you'll regret it if we—"

"I won't. I promise you that. Don't you see? This is *our* time, yours and mine. It's like a precious gift that has been given to us. You said it yourself. No past. No future. Just now. To do with as we choose. Together."

"Together," he said, then his mouth melted over hers.

Dear Reader,

As you head for your favorite vacation hideaway, don't forget to bring along some Special Edition novels for sensational summertime reading!

This month's THAT'S MY BABY! title commemorates Diana Whitney's twenty-fifth Silhouette novel! *I Now Pronounce You Mom & Dad,* which also launches her FOR THE CHILDREN miniseries, is a poignant story about two former flames who conveniently wed for the sake of their beloved godchildren. Look for book two, *A Dad of His Own,* in September in the Silhouette Romance line, and book three, *The Fatherhood Factor,* in Special Edition in October.

Bestselling author Joan Elliott Pickart wraps up her captivating THE BACHELOR BET series with a heart-stirring love story between an amnesiac beauty and a brooding doctor in *The Most Eligible M.D.* The excitement continues with *Beth and the Bachelor* by reader favorite Susan Mallery—a romantic tale about a suburban mom who is swept off her feet by her very own Prince Charming. And fall in love with a virile *Secret Agent Groom,* book two in Andrea Edwards's THE BRIDAL CIRCLE series, about a shy Plain Jane who is powerfully drawn to her mesmerizing new neighbor.

Rounding out this month, Jennifer Mikels delivers an emotional reunion romance that features a rodeo champ who returns to his hometown to make up for lost time with the woman he loves… and the son he never knew existed, in *Forever Mine.* And family secrets are unveiled when a sophisticated lady melts a gruff cowboy's heart in *A Family Secret* by Jean Brashear.

I hope you enjoy each of these romances—where dreams come true!

Best,

Karen Taylor Richman
Senior Editor

Please address questions and book requests to:
Silhouette Reader Service
U.S.: 3010 Walden Ave., P.O. Box 1325, Buffalo, NY 14269
Canadian: P.O. Box 609, Fort Erie, Ont. L2A 5X3

JOAN ELLIOTT PICKART

THE MOST ELIGIBLE M.D.

SPECIAL EDITION®

Published by Silhouette Books
America's Publisher of Contemporary Romance

For Debra Robertson,
Thank You!

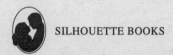 SILHOUETTE BOOKS

ISBN 0-373-24262-X

THE MOST ELIGIBLE M.D.

Copyright © 1999 by Joan Elliott Pickart

This edition published by arrangement with Harlequin Books S.A.

Visit us at www.romance.net

Printed in U.S.A.

Books by Joan Elliott Pickart

Silhouette Special Edition

Friends, Lovers...and
Babies! #1011
The Father of Her Child #1025
†*Texas Dawn* #1100
†*Texas Baby* #1141
‡*Wife Most Wanted* #1160
The Rancher and the Amnesiac
Bride #1204
Δ*The Irresistible Mr.*
Sinclair #1256
Δ*The Most Eligible M.D.* #1262

Silhouette Desire

Angels and Elves #961
Apache Dream Bride #999
†*Texas Moon* #1051
†*Texas Glory* #1088
Just My Joe #1202
Δ*Taming Tall, Dark Brandon* #1223

*The Baby Bet
†Family Men
‡Montana Mavericks: Return
   to Whitehorn
ΔThe Bachelor Bet

Previously published under the pseudonym Robin Elliott

Silhouette Special Edition

Rancher's Heaven #909
Mother at Heart #968

Silhouette Intimate Moments

Gauntlet Run #206

Silhouette Desire

Call It Love #213
To Have It All #237
Picture of Love #261
Pennies in the Fountain #275
Dawn's Gift #303
Brooke's Chance #323
Betting Man #344
Silver Sands #362
Lost and Found #384
Out of the Cold #440
Sophie's Attic #725
Not Just Another Perfect Wife #818
Haven's Call #859

JOAN ELLIOTT PICKART

is the author of over seventy novels. When she isn't writing, she enjoys watching football, knitting, reading, gardening and attending craft shows on the town square. Joan has three all-grown-up daughters and a fantastic little grandson. In September of 1995, Joan traveled to China to adopt her fourth daughter, Autumn. Joan and Autumn have settled into their cozy cottage in a charming small town in the high pine country of Arizona.

THE BACHELORS:

Brandon Hamilton:
Age 35. Hotel owner. 6 ft., nicely built. Black hair, dark
eyes. Principled, protective…powerfully attractive.
TAMING TALL, DARK BRANDON,
June 1999, Silhouette Desire

Taylor Sinclair:
Age 36. Accountant. 6 ft., trim. Light brown hair, brown
eyes. Self-confident, smart, stylish…sexy.
THE IRRESISTIBLE MR. SINCLAIR,
July 1999, Silhouette Special Edition

Ben Rizzoli:
Age 35. Doctor. 6 ft., rugged. Black hair, dark eyes.
Private, precise, proud…purely potent.
THE MOST ELIGIBLE M.D.,
August 1999, Silhouette Special Edition

* * * *

*These bachelor best friends have bet that marriage and
family will never be part of their lives.*

But they'll learn never to bet against love….

Meet Brandon, Taylor and Ben
in bestselling author **Joan Elliott Pickart's**
engaging new miniseries

Chapter One

*F*ree.

She repeated the word over and over in her mind like a mantra, her mood becoming more euphoric with each silent chant.

Dashing among the trees in the wooded area, she stopped to scoop up an armful of the brightly colored autumn leaves that had created a crunchy carpet beneath her feet. She threw the leaves into the air, laughing in delight as some were carried away by the crisp breeze.

It had been over two years—*two years*—since she'd felt so young, so vibrantly alive, happy, and so blessedly *free*.

A cloud moved over the sun that had been filtering light down through the branches of the trees, casting a dark shadow over the woods, and dimming her exuberant frame of mind.

She stilled, wrapping her hands around her elbows in a protective gesture, and drew a sharp breath as a shiver coursed through her.

He would find her.

And he would silence her.

Despite the carefully detailed plan of escape that she had executed, he had power, money, and resources at his fingertips.

He would find her.

He would never allow *her* to get the better of *him.*

"No," she whispered, shaking her head. "Oh, no, please, no."

Panic crashed over her in a bone-chilling wave, pushing aside all rational thoughts. She started to run, tears blurring her vision as she raced on, stumbling at times, then catching her balance and continuing, still gasping for breath.

She heard a strange noise and was only vaguely aware it was her own whimpers of fear.

Scrambling up a huge boulder, she felt the skin tear from her fingertips, leaving droplets of blood on the jagged rock. A sob caught in her throat as she reached the top of the enormous stone, then...

"Oh, God," she said, screaming, the terrified sound carried away by the increasing wind.

She was falling...falling...falling...

Down. Branches of trees whipping at her. Stones bruising her slender body. Tumbling.

Down...

* * *

Ben Rizzoli strolled leisurely through the woods, managing to blank his mind and simply enjoy the sights, sounds and smells of nature's gifts.

He inhaled deeply, savoring the pungent aroma of overripe apples on beds of moist soil and fallen leaves and the sweet scent of pine trees mingled with the last wildflowers of the season still blooming in puddles of sunshine.

A sassy squirrel appeared ten feet in front of him, causing Ben to chuckle as the feisty, furry creature delivered its chattering opinion of his invading its domain, then scampered away.

Birds chirped, others sang in concert, some flew close to the ground, searching for food offerings.

The leaves on the multitude of trees were a kaleidoscope of rich autumn colors: orange, red, yellow, and varying shades of brown. Those that had already fallen scattered in all directions as Ben walked through them.

As each season changed in Prescott, Ben decided that this one was his favorite. But when the next followed, he'd reconsider, convinced that the new treasures of nature were the best there were.

He'd gone through that rather silly ritual during all the years he'd grown up in the small town nestled in the mountains.

Prescott was only a hundred miles above the valley below, where hot, bustling Phoenix was located. But Prescott was a world away from the busy, nonstop city.

Prescott was home. He'd been back almost three years now, having sold his lucrative medical practice in Los Angeles to return to his roots.

But at thirty-five, he was the only Rizzoli left in Prescott. His parents were deceased; his four older brothers and two older sisters living all across the globe.

Sure, he missed his folks, but his brothers and sisters? He barely knew them, the majority having already left home by the time he was born. He had been a *very* late-in-life surprise to his rather dismayed-at-first mother and father, who, at the time, had been grandparents to children several years older than their newest offspring.

He had, for all practical purposes, been an only child, basking in the undivided attention of doting parents. He'd had a wonderful childhood, as close to perfection as it could be.

Fantastic memories, Ben thought, continuing his trek through the woods. Easy to remember these days, too, as some of his best friends from his youth had also returned to live in Prescott.

Brandon Hamilton was back, having restored Hamilton House into a successful, beautiful replica of a turn-of-the-century hotel. Brandon had married Andrea, and they were expecting their first child.

Man, oh, man, the mischief he and Brandon had gotten into as kids, along with their buddy, Taylor Sinclair. Taylor was married, too, and his wife, Janice, had an outlet of her feminine apparel boutique, Sleeping Beauty, located in the lobby of Hamilton

House. Taylor and Janice drove up from Phoenix on a regular basis to check on the store, and all of them—the whole gang—got together to share a meal.

That gang included Jennifer Mackane who'd come home a widow with a newborn son. Joey was nearly five years old already. And cute as a button.

One by one they'd come home. Each having their reasons for returning. Each structuring a life, a present and future, here where their roots were.

Future, Ben's mind echoed, and he frowned. *Don't do it, Rizzoli.* He wasn't going to spoil this picture-perfect walk in the woods by dwelling on what awaited him in the future, the horror of it, the frustration and anger, and the occasional waves of self-pity that suffused him.

"No, damn it," he muttered.

He was learning, slowly, how to live for the moment, to soak it up, savor it, be grateful for it. It wasn't easy to exist this way, not by a long shot. It erased hopes and dreams, and left an empty, dark void within that he prayed he'd find a way to fill with inner peace.

So far, he thought dryly, he was doing a lousy job of accepting his fate. A real lousy job. As busy as he was practicing medicine, socializing with his friends, enjoying solitary hikes such as this one, it was always there, the hard truth, the stark facts, hovering like a menacing monster capable of beating him into bleak and depleting depression.

"Knock it off, Rizzoli," he ordered himself.

He came to a huge boulder, shifted to lean his back

against it, then gazed up at the brilliant blue sky dotted with fluffy, white clouds. There was a crispness to the wind that whispered through the trees he'd emerged from, a reminder that winter was on the way. Snow would fall, transforming Prescott and the surrounding countryside into a fairyland of beauty.

"Then *that* will be my favorite season," he said, smiling at his fickleness.

A bird swooped low, catching Ben's attention. As he turned his head to follow the bird's flight, his gaze fell on the boulder. His smile changed into a frown as he shifted for a better look.

Drops of blood, he thought, touching one with a fingertip. It was dry, but it was still bright red. The trail went up the rock and disappeared from view over the top.

Was there an injured animal on the other side of the tall stone? he wondered. He knew for a fact that there was a steep drop-off beyond this row of rocks. It wasn't a straight shot down, though; the decline was cluttered with bushes, small trees and rocks. If the animal had not fallen far, he might be able to reach it, to help it, to keep it from dying out here all alone.

With a decisive nod, Ben took several steps backward to get a moving start on scaling the boulder, then scrambled up, his hiking boots gaining purchase while his fingers suffered scrapes from the rugged rock.

At the top, he flattened onto his stomach and peered over the edge, his heart immediately beginning to beat a wild tempo and his eyes widening at what he saw more than thirty feet below him.

It was a woman.

Lying ominously still, she was on her back. Her legs were bent to one side, her arms flung out at odd angles.

She was wearing jeans, tennis shoes and a cotton blouse that was torn in several places. Her short, curly dark hair was snagged by the branches of the bushes, and her face was dirty and streaked with blood.

"My God," Ben whispered.

He glanced around quickly, deciding on the safest, but definitely the fastest, way to reach the injured woman. Pushing himself upward, he turned and lowered himself over the side of the boulder, grabbing rough bushes to stop his descent.

Moving carefully, he made his way downward, testing his footholds before allowing his full weight to drop.

What had this woman been thinking? he thought as he continued downward. The drops of blood on the boulder gave evidence to the fact that she'd torn her fingers while scaling the rock.

Already hurt, why hadn't she stopped, quit climbing, gone back down and hiked in another direction?

But, no, she'd obviously struggled to the top of the boulder and flung herself over it, unaware of the drop-off on the other side.

Dumb, really dumb, Ben thought, taking a much-needed breath. Well, that was beside the point. The important thing now was to reach the woman, discover how badly she was injured, then determine the best way to get her back up to the top from where she had fallen.

Slowly… Closer now…closer… Almost there… A few more feet…

Ben braced his feet on the bushes and rocks on the far side of the woman, then tentatively released his hold on the bushes above. Satisfied that he was on a fairly firm foundation, he dropped to one knee and placed the fingertips of one hand on the woman's slender neck.

"Thready pulse," he murmured, then tapped her lightly on one cheek. "Hello? Come on, pretty lady, wake up and open your eyes. This is a heck of a place for an afternoon nap."

The woman didn't move.

"Damn," Ben said. "She's out cold."

A check of the back of the woman's head revealed a good-size lump beneath her silky, black hair that was matted with blood. There was a smattering of blood on a rock directly under her head.

"That answers that," Ben said, frowning.

With hands skilled by many years of practicing medicine, Ben examined the rest of the woman's body, finding no broken bones.

He was probably dealing with at least a concussion, that much was clear. The woman was young, maybe twenty-five or twenty-six, which was in her favor.

She was about five-foot-five with a small frame, very delicate. If anything she was a tad underweight.

She was also extremely lovely, he thought, which had nothing to do with her medical condition, but had definitely caught his attention.

Her features were exquisite, visible despite the dirt and blood on her face. There was just the right amount of womanly slope to her jeans'-clad hips, and the legs he'd probed for broken bones had been slender and long. Small, firm breasts pushed against the thin, torn material of her blouse.

And on her left hand was a wide white circle that indicated she'd recently removed what might have been a wedding band.

Enough of this, Ben thought. He had to stay focused and get her out of this mess.

The woman stirred, moaned, then her dark lashes fluttered.

"Here we go," Ben said gently. "That's it. Wake up. Open your eyes and say hello. Come on. You can do it."

Oh, my, the woman thought, there was a magnificent voice floating over her, caressing her like a comforting blanket. So deep, so rumbly and rich, was this man's voice.

He wanted her to open her eyes and speak to him. Well, that was a reasonable request, she supposed, although she wasn't quite certain where she was, or why she was sleeping in the first place.

So, all right, she'd open her eyes but—oh, the pain, the sudden pain. Her head hurt so badly and her entire body seemed to be on fire and—no, no, she was going back to the dark oblivion, back to sleep where there was no pain.

"No," she whispered.

"Yes," the man said. "I realize you have a helluva headache, but we've got to get you out of here so I can do something about that. I'm a doctor. My name is Ben Rizzoli, and I want you to open your eyes and say, 'Hi, Ben.' You can do it. I know you can."

Dark lashes fluttered again, then the woman opened her eyes slowly, revealing the biggest, bluest eyes Ben had ever seen.

Beautiful, he thought. Absolutely beautiful.

"Hi, Ben," the woman said softly.

Ben's heart did a funny little two-step at the husky sound of the woman's voice, then he smiled at her.

Hi, gorgeous Ben, she thought hazily. Goodness, this man, this Dr. Ben Rizzoli, was so ruggedly handsome. He had thick, black hair that needed a trim, dark eyes, tawny skin and… He was really *very* good-looking in a rough-hewn sort of way.

Well, so much for feasting her eyes on the magnificent doctor. She was going back to sleep and escaping from this terrible pain.

"Whoa," Ben said as the woman's lashes drifted down again. "No, you don't. Stay awake so we can work out a plan to get you up to the top. Tell me your name. I'm Ben and you are…"

The woman opened her mouth to respond. Ben

watched her frown in confusion, then widen her eyes in an expression of sheer terror.

"What's wrong?" he said. "What is it?"

She pressed trembling fingertips to her temples as tears filled her expressive blue eyes.

"I—I don't know who...who I am," she said, her voice quivering. "I can't remember my name or— oh, God, what is happening to me? Ben, I don't know who I am!"

Ben gripped her hands gently, pulling them from her face and sandwiching them between his own.

"Take it easy," he said. "You've suffered a nasty bump and momentarily lost your memory, that's all. It's not unusual, under the circumstances."

"But—"

"Hey, I realize it must be scary not to know who you are right now, but it will all come back to you and you'll be fine. The first order of business is to get you out of these bushes and up to solid ground." Ben paused. "Do you remember where you are? What city?"

She hesitated a moment, then shook her head. "No. Oh, my head hurts so much."

"Well, you're in beautiful Prescott, Arizona, home of friendly folks and perfect weather." Ben released her hands and slid one arm across her shoulders. "Up you go. Easy now. Slow and easy."

A wave of dizziness swept over her as she came to a sitting position and she closed her eyes for several seconds before meeting Ben's gaze again.

"Here's the plan," he said. "I'm going to give

you a piggyback ride, just like when you were a little kid.''

''You're assuming I *was* a little kid,'' she said, managing to produce a small smile. ''I can't remember anything more than waking up here with a roaring headache.'' And staring at the most ruggedly handsome man she'd ever seen. ''This is a nightmare.''

''Well, you'll wake up from your nasty dream soon and be as good as new.'' Ben smiled. ''Ready for a ride?''

''Yes, but first I want to thank you for everything you're doing for me,'' she said, looking directly into Ben's dark eyes. ''I have no idea how I came to be here, but I shudder at the thought of what would have become of me if you hadn't come along and been willing to help. Thank you very much, Ben Rizzoli.''

''You're welcome, Ms.—well, we'll fill in that blank in short order.''

They continued to gaze at each other. Neither moved, nor hardly breathed. Their precarious perch on the side of the hill was forgotten as heartbeats quickened and heat began to churn and swirl, build within them.

Ben became acutely aware that his arm was encircling the woman's shoulders, causing him to lean close, so close to her, his lips mere inches from hers.

Her kissable lips, he thought rather hazily. Beckoning lips, waiting for him to capture them with his own, taste the sweet nectar, delve his tongue into her mouth to meet her tongue and—

Damn it, Rizzoli, he admonished himself, tearing his gaze from hers. *You're a doctor.* This was an injured person and he was behaving so unprofessionally it was a crime.

"All right." He cleared his throat when he heard the husky quality of his voice. "Move slowly, because we don't want to go toppling farther down this incline. Get onto my back, wrap your arms around my neck, your legs around my waist. It's going to be a killer for your headache, but it's the only option open. Ready?"

She nodded and did as instructed, gritting her teeth against the searing pain in her head and every ache in her battered body that the movements caused.

She settled securely onto Ben's back, nestling her head on his shoulder, inhaling the aroma of him in the process.

So strong, she mused. Ben was so strong, so powerful, yet he could be gentle when needed, as evidenced by his voice and the way he'd clasped her hands between his.

Desire. She had felt it thrumming within her when he'd pinned her in place with his mesmerizing dark eyes. Yes, that had been the heat of desire and she knew, just somehow knew, it was different from anything she'd experienced before.

Ben flattened his hands on his thighs and pushed himself to a standing position, immediately grabbing hold of bushes in front of him. He glanced upward at the rough terrain he had to cover, took a deep breath, then started his trek.

"Hang on tight," he said. "I just found you, and I sure don't want to lose you by having you fall off. There are rules about this stuff, you know. I found you, so I get to keep you."

What a stupid thing to say, he thought, making his way slowly upward. She was his now to keep? Yeah, right. For something that ridiculous to have come out of his mouth, it would appear that *he* was the one who had gotten whopped on the head.

But, oh, man, this delicate little lady had definitely gotten to him for a moment there. The heat of desire had exploded through him so fast it had sent him up in flames before he could even attempt to control it.

In fact, he thought dryly, he wasn't in that great a shape right now. Her small, firm breasts were crushed enticingly against his back, and he could feel her soft breath whispering on his neck. Those long, slender legs were hugging him tightly and—

Damn it, Rizzoli, concentrate.

If he didn't give total attention to where he placed each foot, they were liable to go tumbling down the mountain. No way. She'd been through enough. He was here now, making certain no more harm came to her.

She wasn't very heavy, weighed less than some backpacks he'd toted on overnight hikes. But no backpack he'd ever owned had molded to him with such perfection.

I found you, so I get to keep you.

Slowly and very carefully, Ben made his way upward, directing his full attention to the goal of reaching the top. He moved gradually to the right, wanting to avoid the tall boulder blocking the way to flat ground.

Up...up...slowly...so very, very carefully...his precious cargo clinging tightly to him as he made the treacherous ascent.

"Almost there," he said finally, his breathing labored. "Get ready to slide onto the ground."

"Yes, all right."

Five more feet...three...one...

"Made it," Ben said.

She moved off of him and landed with a thud on her bottom on the ground, immediately pressing both hands to the sides of her throbbing head. Ben crawled the rest of the way over the edge and lay on his back, his chest heaving.

"Whew," he said. "I thought I was in decent shape but..." He took a deep breath, exhaled, then turned his head to look at the woman. "How are you doing?"

"Okay," she said quietly, her hands still on her head.

"Dumb question, right?" he said, rolling to his feet. "You feel like hell. Well, all we have to do is get to my vehicle...I'll carry you...then I'll drive you to the hospital and have you checked over."

"I can walk," she said. "You've done enough, definitely above and beyond the call of duty, even for a knight in shining armor coming to the rescue of a damsel in distress. Yes, I'll walk."

"Bad plan, but…" Ben raised both hands, palms out. "Give it a try."

She got to her feet, weaved unsteadily as dizziness assaulted her, then took a step forward. Two steps. Three. Then she began to stagger.

"Oops." One long stride and Ben scooped her into his arms before she hit the ground, one arm across her back, the other beneath her knees. He held her tightly to his chest. "I rest my case."

"I feel so foolish," she said, struggling against threatening tears. "So helpless. And I can't even remember who I am, and that's so frightening, and…" Two tears slid down her cheeks, leaving tracks in the dirt and smears of blood. "…and my head hurts, and my body aches from top to bottom, and you're being so patient, so nice, so wonderful, and—"

Ben kissed her.

He hadn't intended to kiss her. He didn't think it through before kissing her. He simply kissed her, because she was definitely on the verge of hysteria, and he had to stop her before she totally lost it.

And so, he'd kissed her.

Her eyes flew wide open at the shock of Ben's mouth on hers, then in the next instant her lashes drifted down and her arms floated up to encircle his neck.

Oh…my…goodness, she thought, this kiss was ecstasy. She didn't want to think about how scared she was, nor dwell on her aches and pains. No, no, she just wanted to savor this kiss she was sharing with Ben.

Ben drank of the sweet taste of her, while having the irrational thought that he'd waited a lifetime for this kiss. Heated desire was rocketing through him with licking flames, heightening his passion more with every wild beat of his heart.

Heaven and hell, he thought. Sharing this kiss, having this delicate, sensuous woman nestled in his arms was heaven itself.

And the hell? It would come in the form of fury…at himself once the kiss ended.

But, oh, man, his self-directed disgust at his behavior would be worth every rotten name he'd call himself, because this kiss was unbelievable. Fantastic. Sensational.

And this kiss had better be over right now, because he was aroused to the point of pain.

Ben broke the kiss and took a shuddering breath. She opened her eyes slowly and looked at him, causing him to nearly groan aloud as he saw the smoky hue of desire reflected in her beautiful eyes.

Ben cleared his throat. "I suppose I should apologize…I fully intended to, in fact…but I can't, because I now realize I'm not sorry that I kissed you. I just wouldn't want you to think that I go around kissing all my attractive patients. Then again, I wasn't in my doctor mode when I kissed you so…" He paused and chuckled. "Now *I'm* the one who is babbling. Maybe *you* should kiss *me* to shut me up."

She matched his smile. "Okay. It's the least I can do. You kept me from blathering myself into a crying jag."

"Hold that thought," he said, starting to walk forward. "It wouldn't be a good idea for you to kiss me right now, because we might never get out of these woods. You owe me one, though. How's that?"

"Fair enough." She paused, her smile fading. "Thank you, Ben. For everything."

He nodded and kept walking.

Over an hour later, Ben restlessly paced the waiting room of the hospital in Prescott. During the drive into town he'd decided he wasn't in the proper mental place to be the one to examine his damsel in distress.

He'd carried her into the hospital, asked that Dr. Mike Hunt be paged, then handed the patient over to his friend and colleague.

Perfect choice for the physician of record, Ben thought. Good old buddy Mike.

Now he waited, having never been on this end of the emergency room scene before, and not liking it one damn bit.

What in the hell was taking so long?

Mike appeared in the doorway and Ben hurried to stand before him.

"Well?" Ben said. "Talk to me."

"She has a concussion, which has resulted in retrograde amnesia. You know yourself that it's anyone's guess how long the amnesia will last, or how much she'll remember when her memory returns."

"Right," Ben said, nodding.

"She's badly bruised from the fall, and will be pretty sore for several days. I should admit her to keep an eye on that concussion. Unless..." Mike raised his eyebrows.

"Unless what?"

Mike shrugged. "She needs to be wakened through the night, count fingers—the whole drill. Why don't you take her home with you and tend to her at your place?"

"Me?" Ben said, splaying one hand on his chest. "Home? Take her—me?"

Mike laughed. "You sure are a smooth talkin' son of a gun, Rizzoli. Hey, she'll rest better at your place in peace and quiet. Hospitals are notoriously noisy, so why not? Besides, she's terribly frightened because of the amnesia. She's comfortable with you, doesn't feel so alone. I realize it's a tad unorthodox for her to go home with you, but I honestly feel it's the best thing for her. I imagine the police will have inquiries by tomorrow at the latest. Someone will certainly have missed her by then."

"Yes, of course," Ben said quietly. "You're right. She has a life somewhere beyond the woods where I found her. As crazy as it sounds, I guess I forgot that for a moment."

Mike frowned. "Yes, but what kind of existence is it? There's something you should know, Ben, doctor to doctor."

"What is it?"

"There are old bruises on her torso, plus the bruised imprints of fingers on one of her upper arms.

The X rays show a rib that was cracked at some point, and a now-healed broken wrist. In my opinion, some scumball has been using that pretty little gal for a punching bag. All the signs are there. She's been physically abused.''

Chapter Two

Before Ben could reply to the shocking statement, Mike's name was called over the hospital paging system.

"I've got to go," he said. "Listen, Ben, this situation with your mystery lady could get very complicated. If there's a man looking for her, does she even want him to find her? See what I mean? Take her home with you where she'll be safe until this mess can be straightened out. I'll talk to you later."

As Mike hurried from the room, Ben allowed the white-hot fury within him to erupt in a muttered string of earthy expletives.

"Damn it," he said finally, attempting to rein in his anger.

He began to pace the room again, dragging one hand through his hair.

He'd like ten minutes alone with the louse who had been abusing that vulnerable, warm, beautiful woman. Ten minutes to make the sleaze know how it felt to be hammered on.

Ben stopped, planted his hands on his hips and took a deep, steadying breath as he stared up at the ceiling.

Calm down, he told himself, resuming his trek around the room. He couldn't allow his anger to be evident in any way, as it would only upset and confuse her more than she already was. He had to be the same man he'd been out in the woods.

Oh, yeah? he thought dryly. That man had kissed her, and she'd returned the kiss in sweet, sensuous abandon. There would be no more of *that* stuff.

She needed to be protected, not seduced. And damn straight he was taking her home with him. If some yo-yo turned up claiming to be her husband, or lover, or whatever, before she had regained her memory, there was no way in hell he was turning her over to him with no questions asked. Nope. Not a chance.

There were a lot of pieces missing from this puzzle and little by little he was going to put them all together to get the true picture of what was going on here.

"Dr. Rizzoli?"

Ben spun around to find an attractive nurse standing in the doorway.

"Hi, Katie," he said, producing a passable smile.

"The woman you brought in is ready to be released if someone is going to tend to her concussion," Katie said. "Dr. Hunt said I should speak with you about it."

"Right." Ben crossed the room to stand in front of her. "Sign her out to me, Katie. I'll accept responsibility for her care."

"All right. Are you going to notify the sheriff that she's with you? Since she has amnesia—"

"Yes," Ben interrupted. "I'll see to it."

"Oh, be still my heart," Katie said, rolling her eyes heavenward. "Every time I think about the new sheriff the mayor appointed, I get hot flashes. That is one hunk of a man."

"Is that a fact?" Ben said, chuckling. "I haven't met him yet. I saw his picture in the paper when Clyde up and retired in the middle of his term, but I can't say that I was swept off my feet."

"I should hope not," Katie said. "But the female populace of Prescott is swooning en masse." She pressed one fingertip to her chin. "Now, let's see. The new sheriff is from Nevada. He's single, bless his heart, thirty-six and gorgeous. I saw him in the grocery store and, oh, mercy, I nearly died. He's over six feet tall, has hair as dark as yours and green knock-'em-dead eyes. And he's built. Wide shoulders, narrow hips, long legs—"

"Katie?" Ben said, waving one hand in front of her face. "Hello? Where's the patient I'm springing from this place?"

"Who? Oh, and the new sheriff even has a name

that sounds like a sheriff, you know what I mean? Cable Montana. Oh, my stars.''

''Oh, your job, if you don't tell me where my patient is,'' Ben said, frowning.

''Oops,'' Katie said, laughing. ''I was going on a tad there, wasn't I? Your pretty lady is in exam room one. I gave her a scrub top to wear because her blouse was dirty and torn. She's very pleasant, especially considering her circumstances.''

Katie shook her head. ''If it was me, I'd be scared spitless. Imagine not knowing who you are, poor thing. Well, hopefully her amnesia won't last long. 'Bye, Dr. Rizzoli.''

'''Bye,'' Ben said absently as Katie hurried away.

Right, he thought, narrowing his eyes. Let's hope she remembers everything real quickly. Everyone should have the pleasure of reliving in their mind the abuse inflicted on them by some lowlife.

He pulled one hand over the back of his neck, counted to ten slowly, then headed for the designated room. At the doorway to the small enclosure he stopped, mesmerized by the woman who sat on the end of the examining table. She was staring into space, unaware of his presence.

Ben's heart began to beat in a wild tattoo and heat shot through his body.

She was even more lovely than he'd thought. Her face was washed and the leaves and twigs had been removed from her silky, dark curls. There was a bandage on the side of her forehead, covering an injury that probably accounted for the smears of blood that had mingled with the dirt on her face.

Her features were so perfect, so delicate, and there were those lips, those kissable lips that he'd sampled and wanted to kiss again…right now.

She sighed and wrapped her hands around her elbows, jerking Ben from his thoughts. He strode into the room to stand in front of her, forcing himself to smile.

"Well, you look much better," he said. "How's the head?"

"It hurts," she said quietly, meeting his gaze. "I still don't remember anything, Ben. Nothing."

She was so pale, he thought, and there were purple smudges beneath her eyes that said it had been a while since she'd slept well. He wanted to scoop her into his arms, hold her so damn close, tell her that no one—*no one*—would ever hurt her again.

"Don't push yourself to remember," he said. "You'll only stress and increase the pain in your head. Just allow your memory to return naturally. Give it time."

"Why don't I have any identification with me?" she said. "How did I get here? And from where? Was I driving a car? Where is that vehicle?" She lifted her left hand into the air. "Look at this. What kind of ring did I remove? And why?"

"Hey," Ben said, stroking one of her pale cheeks with his thumb. "Take it easy. You'll have the answers to all those questions. In the meantime, you're coming home with me."

Her eyes widened and she dropped her hands into her lap. "I'm what?"

"Mike—Dr. Hunt, who examined you, was the one who suggested it. You need rest, peace and quiet, and that concussion has to be monitored for the next twenty-four hours. You'll be more comfortable at my house than here in the hospital."

"But…" She sighed again. "I don't have the energy to argue the point."

"Good. That will save a lot of time, because I would have won the argument anyway. Let's see how steady you are on your feet." Ben grinned at her. "Hey, I carried you in here, I can sure carry you out again. I've had enough practice at it to be real good at my job."

"Mmm," she said, slipping carefully off the table to stand by his side. And Dr. Ben Rizzoli had had a lot of practice at kissing, too. That kiss they'd shared in the woods had been—no, forget it. It never should have taken place and was *not* going to be repeated. "I'm fine. I can walk."

"I've heard that one before."

"No, really, I feel very steady on my feet." She smoothed the scrub top she wore. "I'm even high-fashion personified."

"Lookin' good. Except I'm not sure pea-soup green is your color," Ben said, chuckling as they left the room. "We're outta here, ma'am, and heading for home."

Home, she thought. It was suddenly just a word that didn't apply to her, didn't evoke any mental images. Home. Where was hers? Who was there? Was anyone worried about her, wondering where she was? Did anyone care?

Stop it, she admonished herself. She'd work herself up to another about-to-erupt crying jag if she didn't watch out. The last time she did that, she'd babbled like an idiot, then...

She slid a glance at Ben as the automatic doors to the hospital swished open and they stepped out into the crisp, early evening air.

Then, Ben had kissed her, she thought as they started across the parking lot. Oh, gracious, what a kiss it had been. She'd responded to him completely and passionately.

Surely she wasn't the kind of woman who went around kissing every handsome man who crossed her path. No, that wasn't acceptable, didn't fit, like shoes that were the wrong size.

Then why had she behaved so...so wantonly in the woods with Ben?

No, now wait a minute. She was being much too hard on herself. She'd sustained a concussion, a physical trauma. And she had been—still was—terribly frightened to discover that she had no memory. It was perfectly understandable that she might act out of character under those circumstances.

There. That settled that.

Except...

Ben opened the passenger door of his large sports vehicle. "Up you go."

"Thank you."

She watched him walk around the front of the vehicle, then open the driver's side door and slide behind the wheel. The powerful engine rumbled to life when he turned the key in the ignition, then they drove out of the parking lot.

Except…why did the remembrance of that kiss still cause heat to thrum low in her body? Why did she want Ben to kiss her again…and again…and again?

Shame on her. She was calm now, had had her injuries tended to, had been assured that her memory would return. There was no excuse for this burning want, this fiery need, centered on Ben Rizzoli.

"Ben?"

"Hmm?" He glanced over at her quickly, then redirected his attention to the road.

"Do people with amnesia behave as they normally would, or might they take on a new personality?"

"I'm not an expert on the subject. I suppose if a person had amnesia for a very long time, they might reconstruct themselves and change in the process. In your case? I doubt it. Your amnesia is pretty textbook—it's connected to your concussion. I'd guess you're behaving as you usually would."

"Oh," she said, feeling a warm flush stain her cheeks. "That's…interesting. I feel as though I'm standing outside of myself, watching a stranger who happens to be me."

"That's an excellent way to put it," he said, nodding. "Try not to dwell on your memory loss. You might remember everything all at once, or get it back in bits and pieces. Just allow it to come to you on its own.''

"I'll try, but it's difficult not to continually search my mind for something—anything—that is familiar to me.'' She paused and looked at her fingertips. "I certainly scraped up my hands, didn't I? It appears as though I've had a professional manicure at some point. I wonder if I could afford to do that, or if I decided to splurge with the grocery money?''

"Hey, don't push it.''

She sighed. "Yes, all right.''

Don't push it, Ben repeated in his mind, because the return of her memory would bring the horror of knowing she'd been physically abused. Lord, he wished he could spare her that, just allow her to exist in a world that began when he found her in the woods. Yeah, that was the ticket. She'd be a woman with no past.

And he, Ben thought suddenly, was a man with no future.

Well, weren't they a pair? Two people living in the moment, nothing more. Strange. They were a matched set, in a way. No past, no future…just *now*.

Ben's house was an A-frame structure of glass and redwood, nestled among tall pine trees. The entire front was gleaming windows that afforded him a spectacular view.

When they entered through the front door, she smiled in delight at the lovely home.

The hardwood floors were dotted with Native

American rugs; the furniture was massive but appeared soft.

The downstairs was open and airy. The spacious kitchen was hidden behind a half-wall; there was a small washroom, an eating area, and a huge, flagstone fireplace on one wall of the great room. And there was a loft where there were two bedrooms with a connecting bathroom, Ben explained.

"This is beautiful," she said.

"Thanks. I designed it and had it built," Ben said, glancing around. "I grew up in Prescott, practiced medicine in Los Angeles, and now I'm back home."

"Is your family still here?"

"No. My parents are deceased, and my older brothers and sisters are scattered from here to Sunday."

"But you returned to your roots anyway," she said, looking at him.

"Yes. This is where I needed to be at this point in my life."

"What do you mean?" she said, frowning slightly. "You look and sound so serious all of a sudden."

"Nothing," he said, forcing a smile. "Prescott is a terrific place to live, that's all." He paused. "Are you hungry?"

"No, but I'm very tired."

"With just cause. Come on, I'll show you to your room and you can take a nap. I'm afraid I'll have to wake you up in a couple of hours, though, and ask you how many fingers I'm holding up. We'll be doing that through the night."

"I'm sorry to be such a nuisance, Ben. You won't get a solid night's sleep."

"Hey, I'm a doctor. I'm used to having my sleep interrupted. I can conk right back out by just closing my eyes. We medical types learn how to do that. I—oh, man, there's the mooch scratching at the back door."

"The what?"

"It's a cat that belongs to my neighbor. This animal calls on everyone in this area and gets handouts. The ridiculous part is, we all feed her. I actually keep her favorite food in the cupboard for when it's my turn to play host."

She smiled. "I want to meet this clever cat."

"Okay, but then you're definitely going to take a nap. It's important that you get your rest."

They crossed the large room and Ben opened the rear door. A fluffy, gray-and-white cat strolled in, her head and tail held high.

"Greetings, Nutmeg," Ben said. "I'm to have the honors today, huh?"

"What…what did you say?" she whispered, grasping Ben's upper arm with one hand.

He whirled around to look at her. "Hey, what's wrong? You're pale as a ghost again."

"The cat. Her name," she said, her voice trembling.

"Nutmeg," Ben said, obviously confused. "The lady who owns her spilled some on the floor when the cat was a kitten and she lapped it up, loved the stuff. So, she was named Nutmeg."

"Meg," she said, her grip on Ben's arm tightening. "Meg. No, no, that's not quite right. No. It's…it's Megan. Ben, my name is Megan."

"Megan," he repeated quietly, covering her hand on his arm with his own hand. "That's very pretty. It suits you, it really does. And, see, you're already starting to remember."

Their eyes met as they stood in the silent room, close, so close, sharing the discovery of her name, testing the sound of it in their minds.

"I'm real," Megan whispered. "I have a name. I exist. I'm a person, a woman."

"You always were a woman, a beautiful, very special woman." Ben heard the gritty quality of his voice, felt the coil of heat low in his body, inhaled Megan's aroma of soap and the lingering scent of a light, flowery cologne. "Welcome to my home… Megan."

She tore her gaze from Ben's as heated desire began to thrum within her, then pulled her hand free from beneath his, shifting her gaze to the cat that was circling around their feet.

"Thank you, Nutmeg," she said, forcing a lightness to her voice. "I'm so glad you dropped by. You deserve an extra treat with the dinner you're about to mooch from Dr. Rizzoli."

Nutmeg meowed her apparent approval of Megan's statement, and Ben went to a cupboard to retrieve a bag of cat food. He filled a bowl with mix, then a matching one with water, and set them on the floor.

"Anything else filtering through the fog in your mind?" he said as he replaced the bag in the cupboard.

Not yet, Megan. Not yet. Please. She had a name now, which was obviously making her feel a great deal better. He didn't want her entire memory to return, though. Not yet.

Why? For her sake? So she wouldn't have to face the grim reality of her life? Or was he being selfish, wishing to have her there, with him, in the *now*, with no past, no future, a while longer?

It was some of both, he supposed. Was that wrong of him? Hell, he didn't know.

"No," she said, bringing Ben from his tangled thoughts. "Do you have any other animals that visit that might supply my last name?"

Ben chuckled as he turned to face her. "Nope. Nutmeg has cornered the mooch market in this part of town."

"Well, darn." Megan paused. "Isn't it strange how much this means to me? Finding out what my name is? It's something we never think about, something we take for granted every day of our lives.

"A name. Who we are. Our identity that validates us. But when it's gone, wiped clean like a chalkboard? It's terrifying. I don't think I'll ever take the sound of my name for granted again."

"I understand what you're saying," Ben said, nodding. "We move through our days assuming a great many things will always be there, never really dwelling on them at all. Things like the ability to walk, talk, breathe, see.''

''I guess as a doctor you've witnessed a great many people losing things like that.''

''Yes,'' he said quietly. ''I have.''

''Well, I'm off to take my nap.''

''Good idea. Your bedroom is upstairs, the one on the left. You'll be able to recognize it because I never make my bed.''

Megan smiled. ''Do you pick up your dirty socks?''

''Sure. On the day the housekeeper is due to arrive, I get the laundry basket, and shovel all my socks off the bedroom floor. It's very efficient, if you think about it. I know exactly where they are when my dresser drawer refuses to produce another clean pair.''

''Oh, my,'' she said, laughing.

Megan turned and headed for the stairs, waggling the fingers of one hand in the air as a farewell.

Ben leaned back against the counter, crossing his feet at the ankles and his arms over his chest as he watched her disappear from view.

''Rest well,'' he said, ''lovely Megan.''

Nutmeg meowed at the door and Ben snapped back to attention to let the cat out.

''See you next time,'' he said. ''Thanks for supplying the lady with her name.'' He paused. ''I think.''

Ben wandered aimlessly around the house, feeling restless, edgy, his gaze drawn time and again to the loft area. As darkness fell, he made a fire in the hearth, then sank onto the sofa facing it, staring into the leaping flames.

His own words spoken to Megan hammered in his mind.

We move through our days assuming a great many things will always be there, never really dwelling on them at all. Things like the ability to walk, talk, breathe, see.

See...see...see...

He jerked forward, resting his elbows on his knees and dragging his hands down his face.

"Ah, damn."

Before it was time to wake Megan, she reappeared, stating she felt much better and the pain in her head wasn't as intense as it had been.

Ben held up two fingers. "How many?"

"Fourteen," she said, smiling.

"Bingo. How about something to eat? I'm not what you'd call a great cook, but I make a decent omelet."

"That sounds delicious." She frowned. "I wonder if I know how to cook?"

"Well, you're not practicing on my world-famous omelets, because that's the only thing I can prepare that's reasonably eatable. Well, unless you want to count peanut butter and jelly sandwiches."

In the kitchen, Ben pointed to a chair at the table and instructed Megan to sit, informing her that master chefs didn't like people underfoot when they did the deed. Megan sat and watched Ben move around the kitchen as he prepared their dinner.

"Ben," she said finally. "I need to buy some clothes, a toothbrush, a comb. If I could borrow some money, I'll pay you back just as soon as I regain my memory and have access to my belongings." She paused. "Heavens, don't loan me too much. Maybe I'm as poor as a church mouse."

"We'll get you what you need in the morning," he said. "There's a new toothbrush in the medicine cabinet upstairs that you can have."

"In the morning," Megan repeated. "Do you suppose someone will have missed my by then, filed a report of some kind?"

"We'll call on Sheriff Montana and find out."

"Sheriff Montana? That's really his name?"

"Yep," Ben said. "Sheriff Cable Montana. He's new in town, and has the women all in a flutter because he's so handsome, or some such thing. Poor devil. He's in for the matchmaking mania that's going to break loose around here."

"Did that happen to you when you returned to Prescott?" Megan said.

"Oh, sure," he said, standing in front of the stove. "I thought I'd go nuts. They gave up on me after a spell, though. Decided I was hopeless, a confirmed bachelor."

"Why?"

"Why did the matchmakers give up their matchmaking?" he said, glancing over at her.

"No, why are you determined not to marry?"

Ben redirected his attention to the frying pan on the stove. "It's a long story. The order of business now is to eat this marvelous cuisine."

Megan held up her left hand and stared at the white circle on her ring finger.

"I think I was married," she said, frowning.

Ben carried two plates of eggs and toast to the table and put one in front of each of their places.

"Was?" he said, sitting opposite her.

"I've recently removed what was obviously a wedding band. What else could it have been?" She lowered her hand and met Ben's gaze. "I don't love him anymore."

Ben's heart began to beat in a wild tempo. "How do you know that? How can you be certain you no longer love him, Megan?"

"I just know," she said, splaying one hand on her breasts. "Love is too important, too all-consuming and powerful. Amnesia or not, if I was in love, my heart would tell me, whispering the message to my mind, my very soul. I honestly believe that." She shook her head. "No, I'm not a woman in love, Ben. I'm not."

Chapter Three

They finished the meal in near silence, each lost in their own thoughts. After cleaning the kitchen, they settled onto opposite ends of the sofa in front of the fireplace.

"It's so lovely and peaceful here," Megan said, gazing into the leaping flames. "I sense... Oh, I don't know...but I have a feeling that my life is *not* peaceful."

No joke, Ben thought.

"Well, I guess that's understandable," Megan went on, "if I recently ended my marriage. A great deal of upset must have preceded my decision." She paused. "I'm assuming that I was the one to seek a divorce. But maybe my husband wanted out of our relationship."

"I'd assume that you set things in motion," Ben said. Because she'd had enough of the creep's abuse. But he wasn't ready to disclose to her what he knew. Not yet. She was too vulnerable at the moment. He'd wait until she was stronger. "I mean, you did say you know you're not in love with him anymore."

"That's true. Well, enough of this gloomy subject. Tell me about what it was like growing up in the small town of Prescott, Arizona. Were you an angelic child?"

Ben laughed. "Not even close. I was…extremely busy…to put it politely. Along with my buddies, Brandon, Taylor, Jennifer, and others, things were never dull. I remember the time we…"

For the next hour Ben told tales of his mischievous youth, causing Megan to laugh in delight time and again. He shifted slightly on the sofa so he could see the sparkle in her blue eyes, drink in the sight of the firelight cascading over her, savor the sound of her lilting laughter that seemed to fill the house to over-flowing.

Megan yawned suddenly. "Excuse me. Goodness, I'm sleepy, despite my nice nap."

"Then it's off to bed with you."

"I'd like to take a shower and wash my hair." She touched the bandage on her forehead. "Would it be all right to get this wet?"

Ben stood, then sat again next to her. "Let me have a look at what you've got there." He pulled the bandage off gently. "It's just a scrape. Pat it dry after you wash your hair. It doesn't need another dressing.''

"All right," she said softly.

Ben shifted his gaze from her forehead to her eyes. The only sounds in the room were the crackling fire and the echo in his ears of his rapidly beating heart.

He allowed his gaze to travel over Megan's face, etching each delicate feature indelibly in his mind, lingering an extra heart-stopping moment on her lips, then looking directly into her eyes again.

"A person should always pay their debts," Megan said, a hint of breathlessness in her voice.

"Hmm?"

"You said in the woods that I owed you a kiss."

"So I did," he said, a husky edge to his voice.

Megan brushed her lips over his.

Like the flutter of a butterfly's wing, he thought hazily as heat rocketed through his body.

"There," Megan said. "Now we're even."

"Not quite," he said.

He lowered his head and claimed Megan's mouth with a quick, nibbling kiss before parting her lips and delving his tongue into the sweet darkness to stroke her tongue in a tantalizing rhythm.

Megan encircled his neck with her hands, inching her fingertips into his thick hair and urging his mouth harder onto hers.

Fire, she thought. She was consumed with the heat of desire that was as hot as the fire in the hearth. Oh, how she wanted this man, wanted to make love with him through the hours of the night.

He was a near stranger, yet she was a stranger to herself, as well. Her life, all she knew, all she felt, was narrowed down to when she'd opened her eyes in the woods and seen Ben.

Ben raised his head a fraction of an inch and took a ragged breath.

"No past," he said, close to Megan's lips. "No future. Just now."

"Yes," she whispered. "Just now. And I want you so much, Ben."

"Ah, Megan, I want you, too. I'm burning with need for you, but..." Ben shook his head. "No, this is wrong. You *do* have a life beyond this moment. I can't—won't—take advantage of you. I'm so afraid you'll regret it if we—"

"No, no, I won't. I promise you that, Ben. There are little clues telling me that when I regain my memory I'll have a great deal of turmoil to deal with.

"Oh, don't you see?" she said, searching his face for understanding. "This is *our* time, yours and mine. It's like a precious gift that has been given to us. You said it yourself. No past. No future. Just now. To do with as we choose. Together."

"Together," he said, then his mouth melted over hers.

Ben refused to listen to the niggling voice of reason in his mind, pushing it away to a dusty corner.

This was now. This was Megan. He wanted her, she wanted him. There was nothing beyond the two of them.

Ben ended the kiss and stood, extending one hand

to Megan. She placed her hand in his and allowed him to pull her up to her feet. He led her to the other side of the coffee table, closer to the hearth, where a plush area rug lay on the floor.

In the glow of the firelight, they removed their clothes, tossing them beyond the rug. The golden glow from the flames increased the sensuous aura, creating a beautiful otherworld essence around them.

Without touching, their gazes traveled over each other, marveling at all they saw, memorizing every detail.

"Exquisite," Ben said, his voice raspy.

"Magnificent," Megan said softly.

They stepped forward eagerly to be held tightly, to feel the other without the cumbersome barrier of clothing.

Ben kissed Megan deeply, then they sank onto the welcoming rug without breaking the kiss, lying together in the warmth of the fire.

Ben splayed one hand on Megan's flat stomach, then moved his mouth from hers to lave the nipple of one breast to a taut button. A soft purr of feminine pleasure escaped from her throat.

"Megan," he murmured. "You must be sore from your fall. I don't want to hurt you. I would never, ever hurt you."

"Shh," she whispered. "Don't worry about the bruises. I'm fine. Just love me, Ben. Make love with me."

He kissed and caressed every inch of her, increasing her passion to a fever pitch. Her hands roamed over his glistening, tawny skin, savoring the feel of his taut muscles, the vivid masculinity of his body. His arousal was heavy against her, and she gloried in what he would bring to her.

"Oh, Ben, please," Megan said finally, a near sob in her voice.

He moved over her, catching his weight on his forearms as he gazed directly into her eyes, seeing the smoky hue of her want and need of him.

"You are so lovely," he said. "I'll never forget this night, Megan, how you look at this very moment, what I'm seeing. Never."

"Our night," she said. "Come to me, Ben, please."

He entered her, filling her with all that he was, then stilled.

"Oh, my," she whispered.

"Yes."

He began to move, slowly at first, then increasing the tempo to a pounding rhythm that she matched in perfect synchronization.

It was ecstasy.

It was coiling heat building with a sweet pain as they reached for release, thundering to what awaited them at the summit of the wondrous climb.

Then they were there, seconds apart, flung far and away from reality to a place they could only travel to together.

"Ben!"

"Ah, Megan."

They hovered, then floated down, down, sated and awed by what they had shared.

Ben rolled to Megan's side, then wrapped one arm around her waist to keep her close. Neither spoke. Hearts returned to normal beats and their labored breaths quieted.

"Thank you," Megan whispered finally. "That was so...so beautiful."

"Yes, it was," Ben said, his lips resting lightly on her forehead. "I've never experienced anything so..." He stopped, unable to find the words he wanted.

"I just somehow know it was more glorious than anything I've ever..." Megan's voice trailed off as she, too, was unable to adequately describe their union.

They lay in contented silence, each tucking the memories away in private chambers of their hearts and minds.

Megan stirred and laughed softly. "I was supposedly headed for the shower."

"You took a detour," Ben said, smiling. "We'll shower together, be good citizens conserving water."

"Indeed."

"The fire is burning low and it's getting chilly in here," he said. "Next stop is a hot shower." He rolled to his feet.

Megan sat up, her gaze falling on one of her upper arms where she could clearly see the bruises from the imprint of large fingers.

"Goodness," she said. "I don't remember you

gripping me so tightly in the woods. Was I in danger of falling farther when you found me, before I regained consciousness?''

A chill swept through Ben and a cold fist tightened in his gut.

''I...um...did what I had to do to get you out of there,'' he said.

Megan shrugged, then got to her feet.

''How's your head?'' Ben said.

''As good as new. Are you still going to wake me through the night to count fingers?''

''I may keep you awake,'' he said, circling her shoulders with one arm, ''but it won't be to count fingers.''

''Mmm,'' she said, sliding one hand through the moist, dark curls on his broad chest.

Ben laughed and snagged her hand with his. ''Enough of that, or we'll never get that shower.''

Megan matched his smile, then they crossed the room to the stairs, walking up them together.

Megan stirred and opened her eyes. Bright sunlight filled the bedroom and the clock on the nightstand announced that it was nearly ten o'clock. She turned her head and saw the empty expanse of bed next to her and a note on the pillow where Ben had laid his head.

She snatched up the paper and read the message out loud. '''Megan. Back by one. Eat. Ben.''' She laughed, mentally saluting Ben's directive to eat.

Her smile faded as she lay perfectly still, searching

her mind, waiting to discover if any of her memory had returned beyond knowing her first name.

Nothing.

There was simply nothing there, just a void, a frightening emptiness that gave no clue as to who she was or why she had been in the woods.

"Don't panic. Stay calm," she ordered herself. "Give it time. Think pleasant, happy thoughts."

A soft smile formed on her lips as she allowed the remembrance of the lovemaking shared with Ben to float into her mind, enveloping her in a rosy glow. Heat shimmered through her as the memory became more vivid, more wondrous.

Ben.

They'd showered together, then tumbled onto the bed, reaching for each other eagerly to soar once again to incredible heights of passion. They'd finally slept, their heads resting on the same pillow.

Ben had wakened her at some point, and she'd dutifully counted the three fingers he'd held in front of her eyes. Then he'd captured her lips with his and they'd made exquisite love yet again.

"Oh, my," Megan said dreamily as she stretched like a lazy kitten.

Her glance fell on the white circle on the ring finger of her left hand and she sighed, her smile vanishing.

Who was the man who had placed the ring on her finger sometime in the past? What had happened to end the vows they'd taken to love and cherish each other until death parted them? Why didn't she love him anymore?

"I don't know anything," she said, pressing her fingertips to her temples. "Except that I'm Megan and...and Ben...is Ben. That's it. That's all."

She sat up and threw back the blankets.

And for now, she thought, walking toward the bathroom, that was enough. During this time stolen out of reality, that was most definitely enough.

Shortly after noon, Ben sat in the chair opposite the desk where Sheriff Cable Montana was talking on the telephone.

Ben narrowed his eyes and attempted to view the new sheriff as the swooning women of Prescott were.

Montana was good-looking, he supposed. He was a rugged, outdoorsy type. Decent build beneath his regulation tan uniform shirt. He was a big man, who no doubt caused the bad guys to think twice before taking him on.

Well, Cable Montana had better rest up, because one of these days the matchmakers were going to leap into action and drive the sheriff right out of his mind.

Cable replaced the receiver to the telephone. "Dr. Ben Rizzoli, right? I've seen you around town."

"Yep, that's me. Welcome to Prescott."

"It's good to be here. What can I do for you today, Ben?"

Nothing, Ben thought suddenly. He was going to get up and walk out of there, not say one word about

Megan being at his house, safe and protected, waiting for him to return to her. Waiting for him to hold her, kiss her, make love to her. Oh, man, last night had been fantastic beyond belief. The lovemaking they'd shared had—

"Ben?" Cable said, frowning.

"What? Oh." Ben snapped himself back to attention and cleared his throat. "Sorry. I'm here to see if you have a missing person's report on a young woman named Megan."

"Megan who?" Cable said, picking up a stack of papers from his desk.

"I don't know. *She* doesn't know. I found her in the woods yesterday, suffering from a concussion due to a fall. Dr. Mike Hunt and I agreed she'd rest better at my house, rather than in the hospital. The thing is, she has retrograde amnesia caused by the bump on her head."

"No kidding?" Cable said, smiling. "Just like in the movies."

"Yep. So far, she's remembered her name is Megan, but nothing more. She might get her memory back all at once, or in bits and pieces. There's always a chance she might lose a chunk of time altogether, too. It happens."

"Interesting." Cable shuffled through the papers. "No, nothing here on a missing Megan." He looked at Ben again. "We can do things in reverse and maybe speed it up a bit. We'll get a description of her from you and I'll send it out over the wires."

Ben nodded. "Okay, but this isn't as cut-and-dried

as it sounds. There's every indication that Megan has been physically abused, although she doesn't remember it, and I haven't told her yet. I don't want her location divulged to the first guy who walks in here, or calls you on the telephone.''

"Hmm," Cable said, frowning. "It could very well be that this Megan doesn't *want* to be found."

"Exactly. If the scum comes to Prescott after you put out the notice, he shouldn't get any farther than this office until you and I have had a chance to talk to him."

"Agreed," Cable said. "I've got no use for men who beat up on women."

Ben got to his feet and extended his hand across the desk. Cable rose and shook Ben's offered hand.

"Keep me up to date on what Megan remembers," the sheriff said after releasing Ben's hand. "Any details are ammunition when and if we question this guy. I'll let you know if I get any inquiries, too. My secretary will give you a form to fill out with Megan's description." He paused. "Good to meet you, Ben."

"Same here. You did yourself a real favor by deciding on this move. It just doesn't get any better than Prescott, Arizona. Well, except for..." Ben's voice trailed off.

"For?" Cable said, raising his eyebrows.

Ben laughed. "You're going to wish you had arrived with a wife and six kids in tow."

"Not a chance," Cable said, chuckling. "I'm going to get myself a dog. Period. End of story."

Ben turned and started toward the door. "Lots of luck. You're going to need it. I'll talk to you later."

For the second time since leaving the sheriff's office and heading for home, Ben swore under his breath and eased up on the gas pedal as he realized he was driving above the speed limit.

Telling Cable Montana that Megan had been physically abused by some unknown man had caused the familiar cold fist to tighten in his gut. The need to see Megan, to be assured that she was all right, was overwhelming, the intensity of it increasing with every passing mile.

What was happening to him? Ben thought, shaking his head. It hadn't even been twenty-four hours since he'd peered over that boulder in the woods and seen Megan lying unconscious thirty feet below.

Yet it seemed as though Megan had been an important part of his life for an eternity, that she was where she belonged...with him.

"You're crazy, Rizzoli," he said. "Certifiably insane and headed for the funny farm."

Megan was knocking him for a loop, that was for sure. Their lovemaking had been far beyond the ordinary, fueled by fierce emotions of possessiveness and protectiveness, and the knowledge that he'd stand between Megan and harm's way at any cost.

He cared for this woman with a depth of feeling he'd never experienced before. Oh, yeah, he was definitely nuts. He didn't even know who Megan was, what her values and opinions were, her likes and dislikes.

Damn it, he didn't do things like this. He was steady on his emotional feet, especially when dealing with women. He never allowed them to get too close, to start to stake a claim, begin looking for a commitment he was in no position to make.

But with Megan? Hell, he was going off the deep end so fast it was making his head spin. He had to get a grip, put the skids on his escalating emotions now. Right now.

"So get it together," he told his reflection in the rearview mirror.

Maybe it wasn't Megan who had him behaving so out of character. Maybe it was the circumstances surrounding this woman who had appeared so suddenly in his life that were throwing him off-kilter.

That Megan had no past and he, for all practical purposes, had no future was creating a sizzling intensity to their *now*. Everything—every thought, every feeling—was stepped up, magnified.

Well, it was time to come down to earth, to burst the rosy, sensual bubble surrounding him and Megan.

He was going to walk into the house, sit her down and tell her the truth. The man who at some point in her life had placed that wedding band on her finger, the man she somehow knew she no longer loved, had physically abused her. The bruised imprints of those fingers on her arm were from that scum's grip, not from Ben rescuing her.

Their *now*—their glorious, unbelievably fantastic *now*—would become stark, and real, and ugly.

"Gotta do it," Ben muttered. "Damn."

He pulled into his driveway, turned off the ignition and got out of the vehicle. Moments later he entered the front door of the house.

"Megan?" he called.

Megan appeared from behind the half-wall concealing the kitchen. She was wearing her jeans, socks and one of his T-shirts, a bright purple Phoenix Suns basketball shirt that fell to the middle of her thighs.

And on her face was the loveliest smile Ben had ever seen. He was consumed by a gentle warmth that touched his mind, his heart, his very soul.

They met in the middle of the living room, reaching for each other, seeking, then finding lips in a searing kiss that fanned the embers of desire still simmering from the previous night into licking flames of passion.

Ben ended the kiss slowly, reluctantly, but kept his arms wrapped tightly around Megan's slender body.

"You're home," she said softly.

"I'm home," he said, looking directly into her blue eyes.

"I borrowed your shirt."

"You look cute as a button."

"I made lunch. Are you hungry?"

He chuckled. "That's a loaded question, ma'am," he said, smiling at her.

"So it is," she said, matching his smile. "Well,

I'll try again. Would you care for a sandwich, Dr. Rizzoli?''

"Sounds dandy, Ms. Megan."

Megan frowned. "I haven't remembered anything, Ben. Nothing."

"Don't rush it. You're doing fine."

Megan smiled again. "I'm so glad to see you. Come tell me all about your morning while we eat lunch."

Ben circled her shoulders with one arm, tucking her close to his side as they headed for the kitchen.

And he'd tell her the raw truth about her life, he thought. Later. He'd do it later. It wasn't something to discuss while having a meal. Then they needed to go shopping to buy her some clothes.

Tonight. Yeah, tonight would be better. They'd sit in front of the soothing fire and he'd quietly explain what he knew about her.

Until then?

For a few more stolen hours, it would just be the two of them…and their *now*.

Chapter Four

Two hours later, Ben realized that he had never before gone shopping with a woman. It was a totally intriguing and fascinating adventure. Megan cheerfully explained her acceptance, or rejection, of various articles of clothing, but to him her rationale made little sense.

The pink sport top was pretty, but the blue one was better because it had one minuscule flower embroidered on the pocket. The green won out over the yellow, due to the added touch of a white waistband. Pastel stripes beat vivid checks, but an equally bright red-white-and-blue number was absolutely perfect.

"I'm really getting into this," Ben said, holding up a purple top. "Here we go."

"I don't want to spend so much of your money," Megan said.

"Hey," he said gently, "don't worry about it. We don't know how long it will take for your memory to return. You need clothes to wear in the meantime." He smiled. "Besides, I'm having fun. How do you like this purple thing?"

"It's nice, but—"

"Sold. You need another pair of jeans, too. You know, one in the wash, one on the body. How about a dress? I'll take you out to dinner at Hamilton House. Yep, you need a dress."

"But—"

"Shh." Ben dropped a quick kiss on her lips. "Don't stress. This is one of the most enjoyable afternoons I've had in a long time."

Megan laughed and threw up her hands. "Okay, okay. You are so-o-o stubborn."

"That's just one of the things we Italians are known for," he said, waggling his eyebrows at her.

Megan brushed her lips over Ben's. "I'm very aware of that, Dr. Rizzoli. Delightfully so."

"Forget shopping. We're going home and locking the door."

Megan laughed and added the purple top to the growing array lying across one of her arms.

It was late afternoon when Megan finally stood her ground and refused to look at another article of clothing.

"Well, darn," Ben said. "I was really on a roll. Did you notice how I figured out what you like and don't like? You didn't reject the last three choices I made.''

Megan frowned. ''Don't you think it's strange that I have such strong opinions about clothes? I guess I remember what my tastes are.''

''Amnesia is strange stuff, my sweet. There are no hard-and-fast medical rules about it. Let's put all these packages in my car, then I'll buy you an ice cream sundae at Hamilton House. You can meet Andrea and Brandon, too.''

When they were settled in the vehicle, Megan reached over and placed one hand on Ben's forearm before he turned the key in the ignition.

''Ben, wait,'' she said. ''Instead of going for ice cream, don't you think we should stop by the police department, or the sheriff's office, or whatever, to inquire if anyone has filed a missing person's report about me?''

Ben started the vehicle. ''I took care of that before I came home for lunch. I called on Sheriff Cable Montana, the new heartthrob of Prescott, and brought him up to date on your situation. He didn't have a missing person's report on anyone named Megan.''

''Why didn't you tell me that you saw the sheriff?'' she said, frowning.

Ben shrugged. ''It slipped my mind. We're to keep him informed about what you remember, and he'll let us know if he receives an inquiry over the wires. I don't think Cable needs to know you like funny little flowers on shirt pockets, though.''

"It's not a funny flower," Megan said with an indignant little sniff. "It's pretty."

"Yes, dear. Whatever you say, dear. What kind of ice cream do you want, dear?"

Megan dissolved in a fit of laughter.

That was close, Ben thought, driving out of the mall parking lot. He didn't want to get into an in-depth discussion with Megan regarding what he'd told Cable. No way. They were having such a good time together shopping for Megan's clothes. He didn't want anything to put a damper on these hours.

He'd stick to his decision to tell Megan the truth about those bruises on her arm tonight. He sure as hell didn't want to, but to delay it any longer would make him guilty of lying by omission.

He didn't want to lie to Megan, had no intention of doing one thing to hurt her. She was too special, too rare, too wonderful.

And although she wasn't aware of it yet, she'd suffered enough because of a man. He wasn't about to cause her any more pain, either physically, or emotionally.

What about you, Rizzoli? his mind questioned suddenly. How would *he* feel when Megan walked out of his life? She'd become so important to him so quickly. How would he deal with the emptiness, the loneliness, the long hours of the night when Megan was gone?

He wasn't going to dwell on that now. Not yet. Next on the agenda was ice cream at Hamilton

House, and that was as far as his thoughts were going to travel.

A soft "Oh-h-h" escaped from Megan's lips when they entered the lobby of Hamilton House.

To step into Hamilton House was to be transported back to the turn of the century, the Victorian motif authentic down to the most minute detail.

A cobblestone path with old-fashioned lampposts fronted a half dozen, small specialty shops that offered everything from flowers and candy to women's lingerie.

"It's exquisite," Megan said, her gaze sweeping over the expanse. "I love it."

"See that shop called Sleeping Beauty?" Ben said. "That's Janice's baby."

"Janice," Megan said thoughtfully. "Let's see. She's married to Taylor Sinclair, who is one of your boyhood friends who helped you torment the town."

"Hey," Ben said, laughing. "I told you…we weren't bad, we were merely busy."

Megan rolled her eyes heavenward.

"Yo, handsome," a voice said. "You need a haircut, but then you always do."

Ben smiled as two elderly women approached. They were the same height, had matching features, but one was dressed in a sedate, high-necked gray ensemble, while the other wore bright red taffeta. They stopped in front of Megan and Ben.

"If I kept my hair in shape, Aunt Charity," Ben

said, "you wouldn't have anything to nag me about."

"Sure I would," Aunt Charity, the wearer of the red dress, said. "I'd just pick something else on the long, long list."

"Figures," Ben said, chuckling. "Aunt Charity, Aunt Prudence, may I present Megan? Megan, these two ladies are Brandon's great-aunts, the Hamilton twins."

"Hello," Megan said, smiling. "It's a pleasure to meet you."

"It's lovely to make your acquaintance," Aunt Prudence said.

"So, this is Megan," Aunt Charity said, beaming. "I just heard the news that you two were smooching in a store at the mall."

"Oh, my gracious," Megan said, a warm flush of embarrassment staining her cheeks.

"Guilty," Ben said, laughing.

"Charity, dear," Aunt Prudence said, "that is really none of our business."

"It certainly is, Pru," Charity said. "Ben is one of our boys. Everything he does is our business."

"Always has been," Ben said, "and always will be, I imagine."

"You betcha, hotshot," Aunt Charity said. "So, tell me, Megan, have you remembered anything else other than your first name?"

"How did you…" Megan started.

"I know everything that's important around here," Aunt Charity said.

"Don't fight it, Megan," Ben said, shaking his head. "You'd lose the battle."

Megan laughed. "I can see that." Her smile faded. "No, I haven't regained any more of my memory yet, Miss…um…Mrs.—"

"Call me Aunt Charity."

"And I'm Aunt Pru."

"Bingo," Charity said. "You're with Ben. You're one of the family now. Don't worry about your amnesia. For all you know, you're better off without all the old baggage you've forgotten."

Aunt Charity had no idea how right she was, Ben thought.

Before Megan could respond further, a couple waved from across the lobby, then hurried toward the group.

Goodness, Megan thought, more people to meet. These two were certainly a good-looking pair, and they were smiling so warmly.

The man was tall and handsome, well-built, and he had dark hair like Ben's but lacked Ben's naturally tawny skin due to his Italian heritage.

The woman was lovely. She had dark brown hair worn in a smooth, blunt cut to just above her shoulders. Her hair was shiny and swung gracefully around her pretty face. And she was obviously pregnant. How blessed she was to be expecting a baby.

A baby, Megan's mind echoed, causing her to frown. It had never occurred to her that she might be a mother. No, no, that didn't set well. She would know if she had a child. She just would.

What she *did* realize, somehow, was that she had a deep yearning to have a baby, a miracle. Yes, oh, yes, she wanted a baby.

"Hey, how are you?" the man said as the couple reached them. "Howdy, Ben, and you must be Megan. Welcome to Hamilton House. I'm Brandon Hamilton and this is my wife, Andrea." He pointed to Andrea's stomach. "And that's the little Hamilton we're excited about. The crummy part is that I have to wait four more months before I can see and hold her."

"Or him," Andrea said, laughing. "Ignore him, Megan. Brandon is convinced we're having a girl. He's also acting like this is the only baby to be born around here who is of any importance. Just smile, nod and humor him."

Brandon and Andrea, as well as Aunt Charity and Aunt Prudence, were absolutely delightful, Megan thought. How lucky Ben was to be surrounded by people like this.

Well, for now, *she* was family, too, and she intended to savor the feeling, wrap it around her like a comforting blanket.

"I'm so pleased to meet you," Megan said. "Ben has told me some wild tales about your boyhood days here in Prescott, Brandon."

"They're all true," Aunt Charity said. "What a handful they were—Ben, Brandon, Taylor and Jennifer. Always on the move and getting into trouble. It's a wonder we all survived."

"They were dear, sweet children," Aunt Pru said.

"Thank you, Aunt Pru," Ben said. "As I explained to Megan, we weren't bad, we were simply busy."

"Yes, dear," Aunt Pru said.

"Ha!" Aunt Charity said. "You were rotten to the core, all of you. You turned out to be halfway decent adults, though, I'll give you that."

"'*Halfway* decent adults'?" Brandon said, raising his eyebrows. "Thanks a bunch, Aunt Charity."

"Wouldn't want you to get too full of yourself, big boy," Aunt Charity said.

Everyone laughed and Megan was consumed once again by a gentle warmth, a sense of belonging, a rightness about standing there as part of the family.

She might not have a past at the moment, but her present—the *now*—was rich, and full, and wonderful. And at the very center of it was Ben.

"We've been shopping for clothes for Megan," Ben said. "And now we're ready for some ice cream."

"Yes, we heard you were shopping," Andrea said, smiling. "And that you were obviously enjoying yourselves."

"Smooching," Aunt Charity said. "That's what they were doing. They were smooching in the mall."

"I know," Andrea said. "Good for them."

"Right," Ben said. "Except the whole town is buzzing about it."

"Of course they are," Brandon said, shrugging. "That's normal for around here." He paused. "Have you spoken to Sheriff Montana about a missing person's report?''

Ben nodded. ''He's up to date on the situation.''

''Enough yakking,'' Aunt Charity said. ''I heard ice cream mentioned and I'm ready for some. Let's all go pig out.''

''You're on,'' Ben said. ''My treat.''

As the group started toward the hotel dining room, Prudence placed her hand on Charity's arm to slow her twin's step.

''Oh, Charity,'' Prudence said quietly. ''Isn't it grand to see Ben so happy, the smile actually reaching his eyes? He's seemed so troubled for months now, but today, with Megan, he's like the Ben we know he can be.''

Charity nodded. ''That's true, but it can't last. Megan has amnesia, remember? She has a life somewhere, folks she belongs with. I fear that our Ben is headed for heartbreak, Pru.''

''Oh, dear,'' Prudence said. ''Oh, dear, dear.''

''Well, don't fret,'' Charity said. ''Forget I said all that gloomy stuff. None of us can predict the future, so there's no sense in stewing about it. Right now our Ben is smiling, and it's a fine sight to behold.''

''That it is,'' Pru said. ''That it is.''

Having consumed huge ice cream sundaes at Hamilton House so close to dinnertime, Megan and Ben didn't go in search of something to eat until nine o'clock that night.

Upon returning to the house, Megan put her new

clothes in the dresser and closet in the guest room, but they both knew she would be sleeping with Ben in his bed.

They chatted about their outing, and Megan went on and on regarding the wonderful people she'd met, telling Ben how fortunate he was to have such marvelous friends.

"They liked you, too," he said, opening the refrigerator and staring at the offerings it held. "How about some cheese, fruit and wine? We can pretend we're artists or some such thing."

"That sounds fine," Megan said. "I only want a light snack because I'm still full from that delicious ice cream." She paused. "Artists…I wonder what it is I do for a living? If I have a job, a career? If I do, surely someone is concerned because I didn't show up for work."

She waved one hand dismissively in the air.

"Oh, never mind," she said. "This has been such a lovely day, I don't want to spoil it by dwelling on what I *don't* know about myself."

Ben shoved cheese, fruit and a bottle of chilled wine onto the counter, then began to cut the cheese into bite-size cubes. Megan came to his side and placed the cheese on a platter.

She'd provided the opening he needed, Ben thought, the perfect opportunity to tell her what he *did* know about her life.

But, hell, he was on the same wavelength that she was. He had enjoyed their hours together today so much, had actually had some plain old fun for the first time in longer than he could remember. Why ruin those memories by informing Megan that she was a battered woman, a victim of physical abuse?

Tomorrow. Yes, tomorrow was soon enough to—

Knock it off, Rizzoli, he told himself. He was lying to Megan with his silence, keeping important information from her that she had every right to know. What he would tell her might trigger some of her memory, shorten the duration of her bout of amnesia.

No! Damn it, no, he didn't want her to remember her existence before the moment he'd found her in the woods. She was his now and—

Man, oh, man, listen to him. He was being so selfish, playing out a fairy tale that wasn't even close to reality. This wasn't how he operated, how he conducted himself. He was grounded firmly in reality; he didn't move through life wearing rose-colored glasses.

He was going to tell Megan everything he knew about her. Tonight. As soon as they were settled in front of the fire with their snack, he'd spell it out. He had no choice. Damn.

Megan carried the platter of fruit and cheese, along with some napkins, while Ben toted two glasses of wine. They set the food on the coffee table in front of the crackling fire in the hearth, then sat on the floor, their backs against the sofa.

Once again the only light in the large room came from the fire, casting a golden glow over them, and the expanse beyond the sofa shrouded in darkness.

Megan glanced around, then smiled at Ben. "See,

Ben? It's like this is our private little world, here in this rosy, warm circle.''

Ben nodded, then took a sip of wine. He set the glass back on the table, took a steadying breath, then shifted slightly so he could gaze directly into Megan's eyes.

"What is it?'' she said. "You're so serious all of a sudden.''

"Yeah, well, I... Megan, look, there's something I have to tell you about...about your life, about—hell.'' He shook his head. "I don't want to do this.''

"Ben?'' Megan frowned as she stared at him.

He covered her hand with his on the top of the table.

"Megan, when Mike Hunt examined you after your fall in the woods, he discovered evidence that you...that someone had been...Megan, those bruises on your arm, the imprints of fingers weren't made by me when I was carrying you up the hill. Those bruises were from—''

"No!'' Megan snatched her hand from beneath Ben's and covered her ears. "I don't want to hear this.''

Ben grasped her wrists gently and pulled her hands away from her head, then he cradled her hands between his.

"Listen to me,'' he said. "I didn't tell you at first because you were hurt, plus you were adjusting to the frightening fact that you have amnesia. But I've run out of excuses for keeping the truth from you. I'm lying by my silence, and I can't do that anymore.

As much as I want to, it's wrong, and I have to do the right thing.''

"No, you don't. You don't.''

Megan jerked her hands free, scrambled to her feet and went to the other side of the coffee table, wrapping her hands around her elbows.

"Your silence isn't a lie if I refuse to listen to you,'' she said, her voice trembling. "You're freed of any guilt you might have. Oh, Ben, don't you understand? In the short time we've been together, we've created a glorious world that belongs to just the two of us, together. It's ours, no one else's. You've made me feel so special, so cared for, so... Don't do this to us, Ben.''

"Megan—''

"Our precious, beautiful world,'' she went on, tears filling her eyes, "is so very fragile, like a crystal ball enclosing us in a sphere of happiness. A ball that could be shattered so easily if we're not very protective of it.

"What you're attempting to tell me might smash our crystal ball into dust that will be blown away into oblivion. Don't do this to us, Ben. Please.''

"I have to.'' Ben got to his feet and moved to where she stood, pulling her into his arms, holding her tightly. "Lord knows I don't want to, Megan, but I have to tell you what I know to be the truth.''

"No,'' she said, a sob catching in her throat. "I don't want to hear you say that Charles hurt me, hit me, that those bruises on my arm are from where he grabbed me so roughly and—''

Ben stiffened, every muscle in his body tensing. He eased Megan away from him, then framed her face with his hands, looking directly into her tear-filled eyes.

"Charles?" he said, his voice gritty as a pulse beat wildly in his temple. "His name is Charles? The man who abused you is named Charles?"

"Yes," she whispered, two tears spilling onto her pale cheeks. "I remember that now. Charles. So angry. So big and strong. Pushing. Hitting. Screaming at me.

"His face...I see his face...livid with fury because I made a mistake. But I didn't mean to, I didn't. I swear I didn't.

"Please, don't hit me again. Not again. I'm sorry. I'm sorry. Please, please, please, leave me alone. No, no, Charles, don't...don't—"

"Megan, it's me. It's Ben," he said, his voice thick with a combination of rage and a sense of helplessness. "Come back to me, Megan. I'm here, waiting for you in our special world. *Megan.*"

She blinked, then a shudder ripped through her. "Ben? Oh, God, Ben." She flung her arms around his neck. "Hold me. Never let me go. Don't let him...Oh, Ben, don't make me go back there. Please."

Ben encircled her with his arms. "He'll never touch you again," he said, his voice low and cold. "I promise you that, Megan. I promise. Do you believe me? Trust me? *He won't hurt you again.*"

Megan nodded, then loosened the tight hold she

had on Ben's neck. She moved back and he released her, allowing her room to dash the tears from her cheeks.

"Thank you, Ben," she said softly, an echo of tears still in her voice. "You are so...I..." She shook her head as emotions closed her throat.

Their eyes met.

Big blue eyes shimmering with tears that reflected the flames of fire in the hearth.

Dark, dark eyes, shifting slowly from icy anger to gentle warmth.

Eyes that delivered and received unspoken messages because of a bond, so rare and special, so deep and rich.

Messages of promises made and promises never to be broken.

Messages of a depth of caring that had become so intense so quickly, that it defied description, leaving awe and wonder in its wake.

Time lost meaning. They simply stood there, inches apart, not touching, yet connected, filling themselves with the exquisite beauty of it all, feeling the warmth of it consuming them, then changing into the coiling, thrumming heat of desire.

They moved at the same moment...messages sent, messages received...closing the short but unacceptable distance between them, unable to bear the slightest separation. The kiss they shared was urgent, hungry, burning with want and need, edged with near franticness.

They ended the kiss, then with hands trembling

visibly, they shed their clothes and dropped to the plush carpet in front of the hearth.

"Our world," Megan whispered. "Our precious, fragile crystal ball of a world that no one can intrude upon, no one can gain entry to but us."

"Yes," Ben said. "But it *is* very fragile, Megan, just as you said, and there is so much out there capable of crushing it."

"Shh," she said, brushing her lips over his. "The longer it is ours, the stronger it will become. That's true, Ben. You'll come to see that I'm right."

See? his mind hammered. Ah, Megan. There was so much she didn't know, far beyond her own amnesia. The woman with no past? The man with no future? The stark truths were stalking them, waiting to pounce, destroy the delicate crystal ball that surrounded them.

Then it would all be over. Finished. Done.

And once again he would be alone. But because Megan had touched his life, been a part of him, for no matter how short a time, being alone would be different from what it had been before.

Being alone would be loneliness.

"The now," Ben said. "Just think about the now."

His mouth melted over Megan's and passions soared. Hands roamed, then were followed by lips, creating a burning path wherever they traveled.

They blanked their minds and savored each tantalizing touch, and taste, and aroma. Hearts beat in wild tempos and their breathing was labored as they drove themselves to the brink of ecstasy.

"I want you so much, Megan," Ben said finally, his voice raspy.

"I want you, too."

Ben joined their bodies in one powerful thrust, sheathing himself in Megan's feminine darkness, then began to move within her.

It was a union even more meaningful than the others they had shared as their bodies now communicated...messages sent, messages received.

They burst upon their glorious place at the summit and clung to each other, once again in awe of its magnificent splendor.

They returned slowly, drifting, separating reluctantly, then nestling together in the glow of the firelight.

Without speaking further, they slept, Ben's arm wrapped protectively across Megan's waist, shielding her from harm, keeping the world beyond the fragile crystal ball at bay.

Chapter Five

Ben lay in bed, staring up into the darkness, his mind a tangled maze of tormenting thoughts. Megan was sleeping next to him, and he envied her the peaceful slumber she was having.

Man, oh, man, he thought, dragging both hands down his face. The cold fury tightened in his gut every time he focused on the faceless man named Charles. He wanted to track him down, make him pay for what he'd done to Megan.

That was stupid. Beating Charles to a pulp wouldn't erase the horrifying memories that Megan had to deal with, wouldn't really solve anything.

There was one bright spot, he thought. As the pieces of the puzzle of Megan's life slowly came together, it was obvious that she was, or soon would be, free to start over, to create a new existence for herself.

Megan would be free to stay by his side, to be with him, where she belonged.

Talk about stupid, he admonished himself, dropping his arms heavily onto the bed. There in the darkness, in the night, the *now* of what he and Megan were sharing was pushed aside by the stark, ugly truth of his future. There was no way to hide from it, nowhere to go to escape from the harsh reality facing him.

He would eventually be blind.

"Damn," Ben said, his hands curling into tight fists.

There it was, the truth, the sentence of doom hanging over his head, the raw fact that meant he had no future, no place in his life for Megan, no matter what her circumstances came to be.

For months now he'd been attempting, and failing, to come to grips with the knowledge that he would lose his sight. He'd made no progress whatsoever in accepting it, finding even a modicum of inner peace about it.

Each time he squared off against his reality, anger, self-pity and fear hammered against him like physical blows, leaving him floundering in a churning sea of depleting emotions.

He couldn't deal with his fate, hated it with an intensity that rendered him incapable of rational thought.

And now it was even worse than before, because

Megan had entered his life. He was getting a glimpse of what it meant to have a wonderful woman by his side. He was registering a sense of being complete, whole, for the first time in his life. When he let down his guard, he'd begin to entertain hopes and dreams of a wife, children, a home filled with love and laughter.

Love. *Was* he falling in love with Megan?

Hell, he didn't know, had no experience to compare it with.

What he *did* know was that he cared deeply for Megan, cared more for her than any woman he'd ever been involved with. There was a depth, a richness, to what they had together that carried it far above the ordinary. Making it so special. So very rare. So incredibly beautiful.

Was this love?

"What difference does it make, Rizzoli?" he muttered.

There was no purpose to be served in struggling to put a label on the intensity of his feelings for Megan.

There was no point in imagining her being free of the damnable Charles, free to live, free to love…him, Ben Rizzoli.

No sense in it at all, because he had no future, nothing to offer Megan. Nothing.

He took a shuddering breath, then rolled onto his side toward Megan. His eyes had long since adjusted to the darkness, and he could see her quite clearly where she lay sleeping next to him.

He sifted his fingers through her silky hair, a gentle smile forming on his lips.

So lovely, he thought. So delicate. She was Megan, with her bubbly laughter, great big, blue eyes that sparkled with merriment, became smoky gray with desire, and tore at his heart when they were filled with tears.

She was intelligent, funny, a breath of fresh air, a brave woman who was taking her amnesia in stride.

Yet when she'd remembered Charles and the pain he'd inflicted upon her, she'd clung to *him,* begging him not to make her return to that horrifying existence.

He was the one she now looked to for protection. *He* was the one she trusted to keep her safe and out of harm's way. *He* was the one she made love with in sweet, total abandon, giving him all that she was as a woman, receiving all that he was as a man.

"Ah, Megan," he said, his voice raspy. "If only…"

No, damn it, the "if only" trip was useless, a futile journey that would only heighten his anger and frustration at his fate.

All he could do was live in the very moment, the now, he was sharing with Megan, one tick of the clock, one heartbeat at a time.

Ben leaned over, kissed Megan on the forehead softly, then settled back onto his pillow. Sleep finally claimed him, but he was plagued by disturbing dreams of being lost in a forest that was menacing and dark.

So very, very dark.

* * *

At breakfast the next morning, Megan was cheerful and chatty, making no reference to what Ben had disclosed to her the previous night, nor her remembrance of the man named Charles. The more chipper she became, the deeper Ben frowned.

"Megan," he said finally. "It's time to talk about last night, don't you think?"

"There's nothing to discuss," she said. "I haven't remembered anything further, so…" She shrugged.

"Has it occurred to you that Charles may come looking for you?" he said, a knot tightening in his gut as he spoke.

"Well, I…" Megan averted her gaze from Ben's and fiddled with the spoon next to her plate. "I just won't speak to him if he finds me. I'll refuse to have anything to do with him."

"Men like that don't usually go away quietly. They're into power, intimidation, control. You won't necessarily be able to shoo him away like he was a pesky fly."

Megan's head snapped up and anger flashed in her expressive eyes. "Why are you doing this, Ben? Why are you intentionally trying to frighten me when I'm working so hard not to dwell on the horrifying facts I've been made aware of?"

"I don't want to scare you," he said, his voice rising. "I'm attempting to get you to face the reality of your situation. Hopefully you've served Charles with divorce papers and he knows you're done living with his cruelty. The thing is, legal documents in his hand or not, I don't think he'll rest until he confronts you.''

"Maybe he already has," she said, matching his volume. "That last ugly image in my mind may have happened, and then I left in search of a place to begin my new life. Did you ever think of that, Dr. Rizzoli? Maybe I'm free of it all.''

"Maybe," Ben said slowly and quietly.

"But you don't believe that.''

"I won't rest easy until we know for certain that that is the way it is, Megan.''

Megan sighed. "I understand, and you're right. I just didn't want to dwell on it this morning.''

"I'm not saying that you should. Just…just don't pretend, don't hide from the truth. Find a place to put it in your mind and leave it there for now, but— hell, I don't know. We need more information. You haven't had the slightest hint of what your last name is?''

"No," she whispered. "Nothing.''

Ben got to his feet, went to the other side of the table and pulled Megan up into his arms. She tilted her head back to meet his gaze.

"I'm sorry," he said. "I turned this into a lousy way to start the day, and I apologize for that. It's the morning after a fantastic night, Megan, and I haven't forgotten those hours, believe me.''

"Thank you, Ben," she said, smiling. "I know you didn't mean to upset me. It's just that…well, I guess I'm doing exactly what you said I shouldn't do. I'm hiding from the truth, because it's so hideous.''

Megan's smile changed to a frown and she shook her head.

''I have so many questions,'' she went on. ''How long did I allow myself to be physically abused by whoever Charles is? What kind of hold did he have over me? Why did I finally have the courage to leave? And leave from where? Have I traveled a great distance? Or am I close to where I used to live. *Who am I?*''

''I know, I know,'' Ben said, tightening his hold on her. ''I'm not helping much, because I keep contradicting myself. One minute I'm saying to just live for the now. Then I'm lecturing you about facing the reality of your previous life. That's not what I would call consistent.''

''No, but I have to make my own decision as to how to deal with all of this.''

''True,'' he said. ''You're a very strong woman, Megan.''

''Am I? There was other evidence of abuse beyond the fingerprints, wasn't there? Wasn't there, Ben?''

Ben hesitated a moment, then nodded.

''There was definitely more than one incident of Charles hurting me. Right?''

''Yes.''

''Where was my strength then?'' she said, her voice rising. ''Why didn't I leave sooner than I did? Oh, Ben, there are so many questions, so much I don't know, don't understand.''

"You'll get your memory back, Megan. All the pieces of the puzzle will come together." Ben paused. "I hate to leave you, but I have patients to see. I have a full day scheduled. Will you be all right here alone until I get back around dinnertime?"

"Oh, yes, don't worry about me. It's lovely and peaceful here. I'll read, rest, maybe go for a walk in the woods." Megan laughed. "Fear not, Dr. Rizzoli, I promise not to fall off any cliffs or..."

Her voice trailed off and her eyes widened.

"The only reason I took that tumble was because...because I suddenly felt Charles's presence and I was afraid he'd find me, so I started to run and..."

"Megan?" Ben said, frowning.

"I remember now. Yes, that's what happened. I was enjoying my freedom, being *free,* then I thought of Charles, of all his money, power, the resources he has to find me, and I panicked. I wasn't far enough away from him. No, not far enough. He was only a hundred miles away in Phoenix, and...Phoenix."

The color drained from Megan's face and she stared into space.

"A big house, huge, very expensively furnished, but cold. A house, not a home." Her voice was flat with no inflection, no emotion. "Gates. Locked gates at the end of a long driveway. A hired bodyguard who followed me everywhere I went. Always there, watching me, spying on me, reporting back to Charles."

A muscle ticked in Ben's tightly clenched jaw as

he listened to Megan speak. He didn't move, hardly breathed, not wishing to do anything to interrupt the flow of memories she was experiencing. The echo of his wildly beating heart thundered in his ears.

"The gates. Locked," Megan repeated, her voice a near whisper. "Scrollwork there. Yes, I see it. On each side is the letter C. They don't stand for Charles. No, no, not Charles. It's…it's Chastain. Yes. He's Charles Chastain. And I'm…I'm Megan Chastain."

"Holy hell," Ben said, not realizing he'd spoken aloud.

Megan blinked at the sound of Ben's voice and he swore silently for disrupting her trancelike state. She shook her head slightly and met his gaze again, her expressive blue eyes radiating confusion and a flicker of fear.

"The name Charles Chastain means something to you, doesn't it, Ben?" she said, searching his face for an answer. "Who is he? Ben?"

"Charles Chastain," he said, then cleared his throat as he attempted to control his rising anger, "is a high-profile Phoenix attorney. He does everything possible to keep his name in the newspaper—he's involved with a lot of charity organizations, that sort of thing.

"He wants the name Chastain to become a household word, because it's rumored that he plans to run for governor. He simply smiles and says 'no comment' when reporters ask him about his political plans."

"Dear heaven," Megan said, a shiver coursing through her. "He's wealthy?"

"Very."

"Then I was right," she said, her voice trembling. "He does have the money, power and resources to find me. He's going to discover where I am, Ben. He will. He'll find me and—"

"Megan," Ben said sharply, shifting his hands to grip her shoulders. "Listen to me. Listen…to…me. He'll never hurt you again. I promise you that. Are you hearing, really hearing, what I'm saying to you?"

"Yes," she whispered.

"*You* are the one with the power over *him*, Megan Chastain."

"What?"

"Think about it," Ben said. "The creep plans to run for governor. There's no way in hell he wants the press to learn that he physically abused his wife. He'd be dead in the water on the political scene.

"One of the choices available to you is that we trade your freedom for your silence. I don't like the idea of him not paying for what he's done, but it would be the safest plan for you, for your future."

"But—"

"And another thing. He won't report you missing through regular channels," Ben rushed on, "because the reporters would get wind of it and have a field day. No, he'll hire a private investigator to find you very quietly. We're one step ahead of Chastain now, because we know who he is and what he's done. We hold all the cards.''

"We?''

"You. Me. Together.'' Ben brushed his lips over Megan's. "Don't forget that. You're not standing alone against Chastain, Megan. You're not alone.'' He paused. "Man, I hate to leave you, but I'm late already getting to the office. Would you like to spend the day at Hamilton House with Andrea and the aunts?''

Megan shook her head. "No, I'd rather stay here. I'm suddenly very tired.''

Ben kissed her on the forehead. "That's understandable. You just had a heavy dose of reality dumped on you. Your memory is definitely returning.''

"Lucky me,'' she said dryly. "So far, everything I've remembered is a nightmare.''

"I know, and I'm so sorry about that. Keep in mind that you're remembering your past, and it's over. The future is yours for the having, to do with as you will. There are just a few glitches to iron out first. We'll handle it. Everything is going to be fine. But for now I've got to get into town before my nurse sends a search party to look for me. Are you positive you want to stay here at the house?''

Megan nodded, then Ben kissed her deeply. He broke the kiss reluctantly, managed to produce a smile, then hurried from the house. Megan watched him go, then sank onto her chair at the table.

"I'm so scared, Ben,'' she whispered. "So terribly

frightened. And there are still so many unanswered questions.''

To Ben's utmost relief, two late-morning patients had cancelled their appointments. He telephoned Cable Montana and made an appointment to see the sheriff during the lunch hour.

In the sheriff's office, Cable sat in the old, leather chair behind his desk. His elbows were propped on the wooden arms; his fingers were tented and resting against his lips. With narrowed eyes, he listened intently to what Ben was saying.

''There you have it,'' Ben said finally. ''Nice can of worms, huh?''

Cable folded his arms across his chest. ''Yep, a beaut. Chastain was news even over in Nevada. He's very carefully paving a path to the governor's office here in Arizona.''

''And Megan could put a real damper on his plans.''

''Oh, no doubt about it,'' Cable said, nodding. ''Chastain's political aspirations would be dead meat if Megan released her story to the press.''

''I'd love to see Chastain get nailed,'' Ben said, a rough edge to his voice. ''But I don't know if Megan is up for that. She may settle for trading her silence for her freedom. She remembers enough to know that she was on the run from Chastain.''

Cable leaned forward, the old chair creaking in protest. He picked up a pen and fiddled with it absently.

"Well, now we know why there's been no response to Megan's description that I sent out over the wires. Chastain is probably doing everything possible to keep the newspapers from getting wind of it."

"I figure he's got a private detective working on finding Megan," Ben said.

"I agree," Cable said. "Does she remember how she got to Prescott? Her car? A rental? The bus?"

"She doesn't know that yet."

"Ben, we have to approach this from the worst case scenario. Chastain is violent, a wife beater. We have to assume he'll stop at nothing to protect his image, and his future plans."

Ben lunged to his feet. "Are you saying that you think Megan's life is in danger?"

"We don't know how far Chastain will go. Megan's safety is priority one here. Better to be overprotective than to leave her vulnerable. You do realize that if Megan would file charges against Chastain now, bring this all into the public's view, he wouldn't dare touch her because all eyes would be on him."

Ben began to pace the office. He sighed and dragged a restless hand through his hair, his frown deepening.

"I'll talk to her," he said. "Explain her options again. She has so much to deal with right now, though. She's getting her memory back in bits and pieces, and none of it is pretty. She can't gather all her inner courage when she doesn't have a total picture of who she is.''

''I understand,'' Cable said. ''Would you stop trekking around? You're making me dizzy.''

Ben slouched back onto the chair. ''I hate this, I really do. I want to confront Charles Chastain and take him apart.''

''Which would result in your being arrested for assault. You might feel better, but you'd be in the slammer.'' Cable paused. ''Look, I'll keep my eyes and ears open for anyone in town who is asking questions about a woman suddenly appearing here. Chastain may have a whole team of detectives on his payroll to look for Megan.''

''Dandy,'' Ben said, shaking his head.

''In the meantime, I'd suggest that Megan stay inside your house with the doors locked when you're not there.''

''Yeah, right,'' Ben said. ''How do I tell her that without scaring her to death? Her emotional plate is full as it is, Cable. How much can one woman be expected to deal with?''

Cable stared at Ben for a long moment before speaking again.

''You care for Megan, don't you?'' he said finally. ''And not as a doctor, but as a man. She's important to you.''

Ben nodded. ''Yes, she's important to me. She's… she's very special, very rare, lovely and—ah, hell. The bottom line is, nothing is going to happen to her. *Nothing.*''

"She's in good hands in my opinion," Cable said. "The best bet is for Megan to blow the whistle on Chastain, call a press conference and deliver the news flash that the golden boy is scum."

Ben opened his mouth to reply, but Cable raised both hands in a gesture of silence.

"I know, I know," he said. "She's not up for that at this point because she's still struggling with the amnesia thing. Just keep it in mind. I suggest you take Megan to the library and go through the microfilm of old Phoenix newspapers. Her marriage to Chastain must have been high profile."

"Mmm," Ben said thoughtfully.

"From a medical standpoint, would it gum up the natural return of Megan's memory if she was given information about herself from an outside source?"

"There are no hard and fast rules about amnesia," Ben said.

Cable shrugged. "So it's worth a try, right? The sooner she has her full memory back, the quicker she'll be able to decide if she wishes to take Chastain on. Personally, I want to bury this guy."

"No joke," Ben said, getting to his feet again. "I have to get back to the office. Thanks for your time, Cable."

"Keep me posted. I'll let you know if I discover there's someone in town asking questions about Megan."

"Okay." Ben started toward the door.

"Ben?"

He stopped and half turned to look back at Cable. "Yes?"

"One more thing," the sheriff said quietly. "Think before you act. Your heart is involved in this, and that could lead you into trouble. Use your head."

Ben nodded and left the office.

Ben walked along the sidewalk in the direction of his office, lost in his own racing thoughts. At the edge of a building he bumped into a huge man who weighed at least three hundred pounds.

"Hey, sorry, Tuck," Ben said. "I didn't see you come around the corner."

"You didn't see *me?*" Tuck said, laughing. "You must have a heavy burden on your mind, Doc. You'd have to be blind not to see the likes of me."

Tuck continued on his way, but Ben remained still where he'd stopped.

Blind, his mind echoed. Blind.

He started off again, his shoulders slumped.

Megan was no longer a woman without a past, he thought, taking a shuddering breath. But he was still a man with no future.

Blind, his mind hammered painfully. Blind... blind...blind...

Chapter Six

That evening, Ben added a log to the crackling fire, closed the screen, then planted his hands on his thighs and pushed himself to his feet.

Megan was standing at an angle to the fireplace, staring into the flames, her hands wrapped around her elbows.

"Megan?" Ben said quietly. "Would you like to talk about it now? You haven't said a word since you told me you wanted to leave the library. If you'd rather be alone, I'll understand, but I don't know what you need from me."

"When I was a little girl," Megan said softly, her gaze still riveted on the leaping flames, "maybe four or five years old, my mother used to take my hands in hers and we'd dance around the living room. She would sing 'You Are My Sunshine,' and we'd twirl and twirl until we fell into a dizzy heap on the floor, laughing, hugging each other. 'You, my Megan,' she'd say, 'are my sunshine. You and your daddy. I love you, Megan mine, and I always will.'''

Megan turned to look at Ben, tears shimmering in her eyes.

"Then they were gone, Ben. My mother and father were gone," she said, her voice trembling. "I was only seven years old. They left me with a baby-sitter and went to the movies.

"Before I went to bed that night I drew them a picture with my crayons. It was a house with all three of us standing in front of it. Mommy, Daddy and Megan. I put it on their bed so they'd find it when they got home."

A sob caught in her throat.

"But they never came home. A drunk driver hit their car one block from our house and killed them instantly. I woke up in the morning to discover that my entire world had been shattered."

"Ah, Megan," Ben said, his voice raspy with emotion as he started toward her.

Megan held up one hand in a halting gesture and Ben stopped.

"No, please, Ben," she said. "Don't hold me right now. I'll dissolve, go completely to pieces. I'm hanging on by such a fragile thread at the moment."

"Then let go, give way to your tears," he said. "I'm here for you, Megan. There's no shame in crying for what was, or for what you've been through.

Having to deal with a lifetime of memories all at once is an extremely heavy load.''

"Tears won't serve any purpose," she said, lifting her chin. "I know everything now, including the nightmare I endured during the two years I was with Charles Chastain." She stared up at the ceiling for a long moment, gathering control over her emotions, then looked at Ben again. "Dear heaven, how I despise that man."

"With just cause. Come on." Ben extended one hand toward her. "Sit with me on the sofa."

Megan hesitated, then moved forward to place her hand in Ben's. He led her to the sofa and they sat down, Ben's arm encircling her shoulders.

"It was the sheriff's idea to go through the microfilm at the library and search for information in the Phoenix newspapers," Ben said. "It did the trick, all right. Slam dunked you with the whole package, snapped you out of your amnesia. What do you think? Should we hug Cable Montana, or hit him?"

Megan smiled slightly, then sighed before resting her head on Ben's shoulder.

"Hug him…I guess," she said. "I should be grateful that my memory has returned. It's just that…well, we had such a special, wonderful, magical world within our crystal ball."

"I'm still here, Megan."

"But now my past has joined us."

"We'll deal with it. Take all the time you need to sort through what you've learned tonight. When you're ready, you can decide what you want to do about Chastain.''

''I was such an easy target for that evil man,'' Megan said, then took a shuddering breath. ''I was raised in foster homes, because there were no relatives to take me in when my parents were killed. I set out on my own at eighteen with little confidence and even less self-esteem.

''When I became one of the secretaries in Charles's office, he must have waited and watched. He knew I was vulnerable and alone. My God, I was gullible. Imagine a handsome, powerful, wealthy man like Charles Chastain being romantically interested in *me*. I was starry-eyed, and innocent, and so incredibly stupid.''

''Hey, don't be so hard on yourself.'' Ben kissed her on the temple. ''You were a victim of a very clever, diabolical man. He figured he could mold you into the perfect wife for a candidate for governor.''

''He didn't love me.''

''No. Any man who hurts his wife the way Charles did you, doesn't even know what love means.''

''He used me, Ben, just as you described. There was a whirlwind courtship, and I was so happy for the first time in years. Then the wedding, the big social event we read about in the newspapers. And then? The nightmare began. The screaming, the hitting, every time I failed to be exactly perfect, the way he was training me to be.''

''Megan, don't,'' Ben said, feeling the cold knot coil in his gut. ''You don't have to relive all that.''

Megan lifted her head from Ben's shoulder to look directly into his eyes.

"Yes, I do," she said. "Oh, yes, I certainly do. Two years, Ben. I suffered that abuse for two long years. I was terrified twenty-four hours a day. Charles had me followed, and everything I did, said, everywhere I went, was reported back to him."

"Megan, you left him. Give yourself some credit. There are women in situations like yours who never have the courage to escape from their hell."

"It took me months to put together my plan to leave, to find people I could trust. It was my hairdresser, Jessy, who was my guardian angel.

"I went to her shop every week, and she saw the bruises, heard the lies I told about bumping into a door, falling down the stairs, whatever fabrication I could come up with. Jessy finally confronted me and I fell apart, just flung myself into her arms and wept."

"I'm glad she was there for you," Ben said, struggling against his rising anger.

"I owe her so much. She made arrangements for an attorney to meet me in the back room of the beauty shop, where I signed the petition for divorce.

"Then on the day that Charles was to be served with the papers, I went to Jessy's shop and she disguised me with a wig and makeup, then drove me to the bus station.

"I came to Prescott with only the clothes on my back. I threw away the wig in the rest room of the bus station here, washed my face and set out. I ended up in the woods, feeling so free, so blessedly free.''

''You didn't have any identification with you?'' Ben said.

''No, nothing. I put money in the pocket of my jeans. It must have fallen out when I tumbled down that hill.''

''And I found you,'' Ben said, managing to produce a smile.

Megan brushed her lips over Ben's.

''So you did,'' she said, matching his small smile. ''I'll never forget the moment I opened my eyes and saw you for the first time, nor everything we've shared since.

''Being with you, Ben, is the purest happiness I've experienced since my mother sang 'You Are My Sunshine,' and danced with me while she held my hands.''

''These memories are ours to keep,'' Ben said. ''No matter what happens in the future.''

Future? his mind taunted. Damn it, he didn't have one worth talking about.

''Goodness, we sound so gloomy,'' Megan said. ''As though everything we have together is over. It's just that…well, I'm no longer Megan with no past. I'm Megan Chastain, who has a great deal of baggage in my life. You're surely viewing me through different eyes, and I understand why you would.''

''No, I—''

''Shh,'' she said, placing two fingertips on his lips for a moment. ''It's all right, Ben. Reality has entered our private world, and if you'd prefer, I can stay somewhere else.'' She frowned. ''That's cute. I don't have any money. I really should start looking for a job.''

''Would you stop it?'' Ben said, shifting to grip her by the shoulders. ''You're being awfully quick to dust me off. I want you to stay right here, with me. Not only that, you're to keep the doors locked when I'm not home. Don't go for any more walks outside, either.''

''Listen to what you're saying, Ben. You're assuming Charles is dangerous, and will stop at nothing to find me and be assured of my silence about the kind of man he really is. I can't ask you to be involved in a terrible situation like this one.''

''You're *not* asking, nor is it open for discussion. I have every intention of seeing you through this entire mess, Megan.''

Ben dropped his hands from her shoulders and gave her a quick kiss.

And then? Megan wondered. Where were they headed, she and Ben? What would the future bring? She cared so very much for him, might even be falling in love with him, for all she knew.

''All I know is, my life is extremely complicated, possibly even dangerous. Your life? It's so serene and peaceful, with no worries, no woes. Our...our relationship is very out of balance.''

Ben got to his feet and went to the hearth, shoving his hands into the back pockets of his jeans as he stared into the crackling flames of the fire.

"Things aren't always as they appear, Megan," he said quietly, keeping his back to her. "I'm not without baggage, either, but this isn't the time to get into it. We have enough to deal with right now. You need to be giving thought to whether you intend to blow the whistle on Chastain."

Megan frowned as she stared at Ben's broad back.

Ben *did* have worries and woes, she thought. There was something he wasn't telling her, something of extreme importance. It was as though he'd suddenly built a wall around himself, was shutting her out.

Oh, Ben, what is it? What's plaguing you? What aren't you sharing with me?

"Ben?"

He turned to face her, squaring his shoulders in the process and producing a smile that didn't quite reach his eyes.

"Well, pretty lady, it's getting late. Enough heavy talk for one night."

Megan sighed. "It's no longer possible to just live for the now, is it?"

"No," he said. "It's no longer possible."

Megan nodded and got to her feet.

Their lovemaking that night had an urgent quality to it, a need to hold fast to each other, escape into the wondrous place their union would take them to. They didn't want to think, only wished to feel, savor...and soar...to exquisite ecstasy.

The next evening, Ben told Megan to put on the pretty dress they'd bought and he would take her to dinner at Hamilton House. At the hotel, an attractive woman greeted them as they entered the dining room.

"Megan," Ben said. "This is Jennifer Mackane."

"Oh, yes, of course," Megan said, smiling. "You were part of the group who kept everyone on their toes when you were children here in Prescott."

Jennifer laughed, the sound lovely and lilting. She appeared to be in her early thirties, had a nice figure, and her hair was a tumble of shoulder-length, strawberry-blond waves. Her green eyes sparkled with merriment.

"What a reputation we all have," she said, smiling. "If my son, Joey, follows in my footsteps, he'll put me in an early grave." She paused. "It's marvellous to meet you, Megan. I'm the manager of this dining room and I have a special table for you and Ben."

"How's Joey?" Ben said.

"Driving me nuts," Jennifer said. "He's so excited about his birthday party on Saturday, he's jumping out of his shoes. He's practicing saying 'I'm five years old' at the top of his lungs. You're coming to the party, aren't you, Ben? Megan, are you up for a five-year-old's big day? We'd love to have you attend."

"Thank you," Megan said. "It sounds like fun."

"No, it will be bedlam," Jennifer said, laughing again. "Come on, I'll show you to your table."

When Megan and Ben were seated, Jennifer

handed them two oversize menus. She bent down and lowered her voice.

"Are you ready for this?" she said. "Aunt Charity has informed me that Sheriff Montana and I would make a perfect couple because we both have green eyes."

"Ah, the matchmaking for Cable Montana begins," Ben said, chuckling. "Hey, why not, Jennifer? People have gotten together for less sensible reasons than having the same color eyes. I like Cable. He's a good man."

"I'm sure he is," Jennifer said. "But I'm not interested, thank you very much. The only member of the male species I need in my life will be five years old on Saturday. Besides, I've already suffered through the matchmaking bit, and was declared officially hopeless. Cable Montana is on his own. I wish him luck."

"He'll need it." Ben shook his head. "Big time."

"That's the truth," Jennifer said, laughing. "Well, duty calls. It was great meeting you, Megan. Enjoy your dinner, you two."

As Jennifer walked away, Megan frowned slightly.

"What a charming, vivacious woman Jennifer is," she said. "I'm assuming from what she said that she's a single mother, yet she's definitely not interested in having a relationship with a man."

Ben shook his head. "No, she's not. Jennifer was widowed a week before Joey was born when her husband, Joe, was killed in a construction accident. Jennifer chose to move back here with her newborn son to raise him where she grew up.''

"How tragic to have been widowed so young, and at what should have been such a happy time in her marriage. She named the baby after her husband, so they must have been very happy together. I would guess...I don't know...that Jennifer feels she could never duplicate what she had with her Joe.''

"Maybe that's the reason she refuses even to date," Ben said, nodding. "It would mean, though, that Jennifer is living in the past, instead of moving forward. She has a lot to offer a man, and Joey would be a fantastic bonus for some lucky guy. Jennifer needs to let go of what was, and concentrate on what might yet be.''

"Would you give that same advice to me?" Megan said.

"You're already doing that, Megan. If you weren't, if you were afraid to be close to a man because he might suddenly erupt in anger and—well, let's just say I really respect your strength and courage. If you were allowing Chastain to still have control over you, you wouldn't..." Ben's voice trailed off as he glanced around quickly.

"I wouldn't be capable of making love with you," Megan said very softly so only Ben could hear.

He nodded.

"But I'm not entirely free of the past," Megan said, sighing. "I still have to close the final door on my life with Charles.''

"Yes, you do," Ben said. "You have to decide if you want to go public with the truth about Chastain."

"Well, I don't have to think about that tonight." Megan swept her gaze over the room. "In fact, I can't, because I've been transported back in time to the turn of the century. I'm…let's see here…yes, I'm the teacher in a one-room schoolhouse in Prescott."

"Oh, okay," Ben said, chuckling. "And who am I, pray tell?"

"The country doctor, of course. You do everything from setting broken arms to delivering babies. You often take your pay in eggs, chickens, and fresh produce. You travel the land in a horse and buggy."

"Is that a fact?" Ben said, still smiling. "As a general practitioner, that about covers what I do now. The horse and buggy part sounds grim, though. I suppose it's quite scandalous that the doctor and the teacher are having dinner together."

"Oh, my, yes," Megan said, matching Ben's smile. "Tongues are wagging."

"My dear Megan, tongues are wagging about us in present-day Prescott. Some things don't change."

"No," Megan said, suddenly serious. "But some things *do* change, and for the better. Like my life. I'm so glad you found me that day in the woods, Ben."

"So am I, Megan," he said quietly.

Their eyes met and desire began to build within them, hot and pulsing. The room faded into a hazy mist as they saw only each other, along with vivid, sensual images in their minds of lovemaking shared and lovemaking yet to come.

"Would you care to see a wine list?" a young man said, appearing at the side of their table.

Ben and Megan jerked in their chairs at the sudden intrusion into the sensuous place they'd floated to together.

"Cripes, George," Ben said. "Scare me to death, why don't you?"

"Hi, Doc," George said. "I cleared my throat, but you were a hundred miles away. So, do you want some wine or what?"

"Sure," Ben said, accepting the list George extended toward him. "This is a special night."

"Oh, yeah?" George said. "What are you two celebrating?"

"Just being here," Ben said.

"Right," George said, eyeing him warily. "Whatever you say, Doc."

Just being here, Megan mentally repeated as Ben conducted business with George. In the now. But what about the future? What did it hold? And what disturbing secret was Ben keeping from her?

No, Megan, don't, she admonished herself. She wasn't going to allow anything to spoil this lovely evening, these precious moments spent with Ben.

Hours later, Ben bolted upright in bed, suddenly wide awake. He waited for his thundering heart to quiet, then listened intently for any sound in the house that might have jarred him from his sleep.

There was nothing but the deep silence of a peaceful night. He looked at Megan where she lay sleeping next to him and knew why he was awake and feeling so unsettled, so disturbed.

Ben dragged both hands down his face.

He'd had a dream. A dream that had been so vivid, so real, he was still having difficulty pushing the images from his mind.

He and Megan had been here, in this house. Sunlight had poured through the front windows like a warm, golden waterfall that flowed over them with a gentle touch.

They'd been sitting on the rug in front of the hearth, and on a fluffy blanket spread out between them was a baby—*their* baby. The infant had dark hair and eyes, and was kicking tiny feet in the air and waving minuscule fists.

Sunlight glimmered off matching gold wedding bands on his and Megan's hands. They were smiling at each other, love shining in their eyes, then they gazed at the miracle they'd created together...their child.

It had been so perfect, all of it, there in the dream. There in the future.

And none of it was possible.

With a groan, Ben threw back the blankets and left the bed. He pulled on a pair of jeans and went downstairs, forcing himself to go to the rug in front of the hearth, to stare at its emptiness.

Damn it, he fumed, couldn't he escape from the

truth of his fate even while he slept? Was there nowhere left to hide from the harsh reality of his future?

That dream. Had it been his subconscious rising through the depths of slumber to produce in crystal clarity his hopes, dreams, what he really wanted, needed? Was he falling in love with Megan? Envisioning her as his wife, the mother of his child, in his heart, his very soul?

"What difference does it make?" he said aloud, a rough edge to his voice.

It didn't matter what his innermost yearnings might be. He was a man without choices to make. His destiny was out of his hands and nothing would change that.

But as each minute, hour, day, and night passed with Megan by his side, he was pushing the truth further away, refusing to address it or acknowledge that it was there.

That was wrong. So damn wrong.

Ben spun around and strode across the room to the kitchen. He yanked a tea towel from one of the drawers, folded it into a strip and tied it behind his head, covering his eyes.

A shiver coursed through him as he was engulfed in darkness.

With his arms waving back and forth in front of him, he made his way forward, then slammed into the kitchen table. He swore under his breath and turned, inching his way into the main room of the house. His heart beat in a wild rhythm and a trickle of sweat ran down his chest.

He bumped into the couch, then kept one hand sliding along the top, his other arm sweeping through the air.

Dark. So dark. So terrifyingly dark. This room that should be so familiar was suddenly an unknown place of danger, of obstacles waiting to trip him up, to cause him to stagger and whimper like a frightened child in the night.

This was his future, he thought fiercely, forcing himself to keep moving. There was no Megan here in the darkness. No baby. No sunlight and warmth. There was only a cold, black eternity of helplessness.

Megan stood at the railing to the loft area, her fingertips pressed to her lips as she watched Ben.

What was he doing? Why had he covered his eyes…as though he was *blind.*

Megan's breath caught and her eyes widened as she continued to stare at Ben's unsteady trek across the room.

Was that the secret Ben was keeping from her? Was that what he refused to share? Was Ben Rizzoli going blind?

On trembling legs, Megan made her way down the stairs, clad in panties and one of Ben's T-shirts. She stopped at the bottom, her heart aching as she watched Ben's cautious journey on shuffling feet.

"Ben?" she said softly.

Ben halted, every muscle in his body tensing to the point of pain as he heard Megan speak his name. He sucked in a shuddering breath, then turned in the direction of her voice, leaving the towel over his eyes.

"Enjoy the show, Megan?" he said, his voice harsh. "Nice performance, huh? A toddler learning to walk has enough sense not to barrel into furniture like an idiot. But I'm a man, aren't I? A big, brave, tough guy who isn't supposed to be afraid of anything. What a joke. I can't even get across the room, let alone slay dragons."

"Ben, what—"

"This is my reality!" Ben shouted, tearing the towel from his eyes and flinging it away. "How do you like that, Megan? We were perfect together when you had no past, because I have no future. We had only the now and it was…it was…" He shook his head and stared up at the ceiling for a long moment. "Forget it."

Megan started toward him. "Ben, I don't understand. What's happening to you? Talk to me."

Ben raised one hand. "Don't come near me. I can't think straight when you're close to me, when I'm holding you, making love with you. Hopes, dreams, ridiculous visions of a future become bigger, brighter than the stark darkness of my truth. *Stay…away…from me.*"

Megan cringed as the loud, rough volume of Ben's voice seemed to strike her like a physical blow. She wrapped her shaking hands around her elbows and took a staggering step backward.

She blinked, the color draining from her face as

the image of an angry Charles was superimposed over Ben, causing a sob to escape from her throat.

"I'm sorry," she said, her voice quivering. "I didn't mean to upset you, I swear I didn't. Please forgive me, Charles." Tears filled her eyes. "Oh, don't...don't...don't..."

Megan retreated farther, bumping into the stairs and losing her balance, sprawling onto her back on the steps. She attempted to curl into a ball, flinging her arms wildly toward the staircase rungs, then gripping them tightly.

"No-o-o," she screamed. "Charles, please no!"

"My God," Ben said in a hoarse whisper. "What have I done?"

He ran across the room and reached out to Megan. She pulled away, drawing her knees up further and burying her head in her lap.

"Megan, I'm sorry. It's me, Ben. It's Ben, Megan, and I'm not going to hurt you. I'm so, so sorry." He placed one hand on her back, tentatively, gently. "Listen to my voice, sweetheart. It's me. It's Ben. Everything is all right. You have nothing to be afraid of. Megan?"

A second ticked by. Then two...three.

"Ben?" Megan whispered finally.

"Yes, it's me. Forgive me, please, for frightening you. I would never hurt you, Megan. Never."

Megan raised her head and Ben groaned deep in his chest when he saw her pale cheeks glistening with tears, saw the stark terror in the depths of her big, blue eyes.

He scooped her into his arms and sat on the floor at the bottom of the stairs, Megan across his lap. He held her tightly, rocking back and forth as though she was a small child.

She clung to him, one last shudder rippling through her before she finally relaxed and leaned into him. He stilled, sinking his face into her dark, silken curls.

The silvery moonlight poured over them as they sat there, not moving, hardly breathing, each warring with inner ghosts and fears, each seeking solace from the one they held so close, refusing to let go.

Chapter Seven

Megan was still sleeping when Ben left the house the next morning to go to his office. As he drove away from the house, he rotated his neck back and forth, aware that he was bone-weary even before his busy day began.

He had no idea how long he had sat on the floor the previous night with Megan held tightly in his arms. Time had lost meaning. They had both been drained, emotionally exhausted, after what had taken place.

Megan had dozed finally and Ben had leveled himself to his feet and carried her up the stairs to bed.

"Ben," she had murmured. "Please share with me. Tell me what is happening to you."

"Shh," he had said gently. "Tomorrow. I'll explain everything to you tomorrow. Just sleep now, Megan.''

Ben's grip on the steering wheel tightened and he frowned deeply as he remembered the moment when he had frightened Megan so badly, she'd been transported back in time, to relive the abuse she'd suffered at the hands of Charles Chastain.

''Damn it,'' he said, smacking one hand against the steering wheel.

Megan had forgiven him already, trusted him again, had allowed him to touch her, hold her in his arms. What an incredible and rare woman she was. He was so angry at himself for what he had done, he didn't feel he deserved her devotion and trust.

What a mess. Now *his* reality was demanding space in his and Megan's special, crystal ball world.

He'd promised he would tell her what he was facing, the stark facts of his hopeless future. He'd keep that promise, because he was a man of his word.

And then what? Hell, that would be that. Megan would realize he had nothing to offer her. She'd concentrate on obtaining closure to her situation with Chastain, then she'd leave to begin her new life as a free woman.

What he and Megan had together would be over. Finished. Done.

He'd face his bleak future alone. Face the impending darkness, the terrifying nothingness, alone.

''That's how it was before I found Megan in the woods,'' he said aloud, a rough edge to his voice. ''That's how it will be again.''

Except...

He was different now, changed. Because of Megan, he'd foolishly opened an emotional door that illuminated hopes and dreams, wants and needs, bringing them into crystal clarity.

Closing that door again, locking it tightly, was going to be tough and very painful. And it would deepen the intensity of the darkness.

He was living on borrowed time with Megan. He'd known that from the beginning, but he had continually pushed that reality away. He could no longer do that, because when he returned home tonight, he would spell out everything to Megan, put it all on the table for her to see.

"See," Ben said with a snort of disgust. "The magic word. The word from hell."

He drew a deep breath and exhaled slowly.

He had to get his act together. The patients he would tend to today deserved his full concentration and expertise.

Ben parked his vehicle in the back of the small building that housed his office, went to the rear door and unlocked it. He strode down the hall to the reception area.

His secretary, Cynthia, was chatting with his nurse, Sharon, as they sipped from mugs of freshly brewed coffee. Both women were widows in their late fifties. Both were top-notch in their jobs and were dedicated to Ben and the patients who believed in him.

"'Morning, ladies." Ben tried for a lighthearted tone. "How goes it?"

"Hi, Ben," they said in unison.

"How much time do I have before the first patient arrives?" he said.

Cynthia glanced at the appointment book. "Fifteen minutes."

"Good," he said. "I have to make a telephone call."

"I'll buzz you when we need you," Cynthia said. "Coffee is hot."

"Thanks," Ben said.

"How's Megan?" Sharon said.

"Doin' fine," Ben said, starting back down the hall.

Yeah, right, he thought dryly. Megan was fine when he wasn't scaring the hell out of her. She was fine when she didn't dwell on the decision she had to make regarding Charles Chastain. But she wouldn't be even close to fine after he spilled his guts to her tonight and divulged the truth about himself.

"Yep," he repeated, loud enough for the women to hear. "Doin' fine."

Ben sank onto the soft leather chair behind his desk, put down the coffee mug and placed one hand on the receiver to the telephone. He hesitated, then forced himself to lift the receiver and punch in numbers he knew by heart, despite the fact that he hadn't used them in months.

A few moments later he had identified himself and asked to speak to Dr. Fred Bolstad. Ben drummed his fingers on the desktop as recorded music hummed in his ear when he was placed on hold.

"Come on. Come on," he muttered.

"Ben," a deep voice said finally. "It's been a long time. How are you?"

"Doin' fine," Ben said, then rolled his eyes heavenward. "Listen, Fred, I know you're busy and... well, I just needed to check in with you on the outside chance that—hell, this is stupid. If you had anything to tell me, you would have called."

"Hey, no problem. I understand your need to touch base. I'm still researching your situation every chance I get, but...well, there's nothing new to report."

"Right. I won't keep you. Thanks for—"

"Ben, wait," Fred interrupted. "I really wish you'd get me an update on your brothers."

"What's the point, Fred?" Ben said, a pulse beginning to beat wildly in his temple. "My father went blind. My oldest brother is blind. My next oldest brother was losing his sight the last time I spoke with him.

"The deck is stacked. It's just a matter of time until it's my turn. My sisters, who are older than any of us guys, are fine. This...whatever it is...is being passed down to the male Rizzolis."

"And all my months of research haven't revealed the gene that's doing it," Fred said. "That happens often enough to give researchers like me ulcers.

Some things just don't surface even in the most sophisticated DNA testing. There's nothing to give us a clue as to why this is happening. Damn, it's frustrating. We sure as hell can't treat what we can't find.''

"I know," Ben said quietly.

"Have you had any symptoms?" Fred said. "Blurred or double vision, trouble seeing at night, black dots in front of your eyes, headaches? Any of the things your oldest brother told you about?"

"No, nothing at all so far."

"Good, that's good." Fred paused. "Ben, please, humor me. Get me an update on your brothers, will you?"

"Yeah, yeah, okay, for all the good it will do. I've been playing ostrich on that, I guess. I didn't want to hear their bad news, but I'll give them a call. I'll get back to you, Fred."

"Take it easy, man."

"Sure. 'Bye, Fred."

Ben replaced the receiver, sank back in his chair, and dragged his hands down his face.

"Ah, Megan," he said, his voice thick with emotion. "I'm so damn sorry."

Well, that was a switch, he thought, lunging to his feet. For the first time, he was feeling more badly for someone other than himself regarding this disaster. For Megan. Who made him feel wonderful, complete, whole. His other half.

His soul mate?

The woman he was in love with?

"Forget it," he said. "I don't want to know the answer to *that* one."

To Megan, the day seemed like an endless stretch of hours as she waited for Ben to return home. Every time she glanced at the clock she frowned, wondering if it was actually working. Ben had told her to remain in the house with the doors locked, and had what she knew was a ridiculous, psychological urge to be outside in the crisp, fresh air.

She sighed, told herself she was tired of hearing the pitiful sound, then flopped down on the sofa.

One more hour, she thought. Ben would be home in one hour, providing he didn't have any late, unexpected patients arrive at his office.

She'd made some stew that was simmering on the stove, the rich aroma filling the house. She was not, however, one bit hungry, due to the knot in her stomach that had been there the entire day.

Megan sighed again, clicked her tongue in self-disgust, then leaned her head back on the top of the sofa. She stared at the ceiling and replayed in her mind, for the umpteenth time, the events of the previous night.

What a nightmare it had all been, how terrifying. Ben was going to explain everything to her, but it was obvious from what had taken place that Ben Rizzoli was going blind. He was angry, with just cause, and no doubt frightened about what he was facing in the future.

Ben had needed her to comfort him, hold him, be

strong for him, as he'd been for her so many times as she'd come to grips with her past.

But had she been there for him? Oh, no, not her. Her ghosts had been too powerful, too strong, had rendered her helpless, a weeping, shivering mess, who once again clung to Ben for solace and safety.

She had let Ben down and she was so ashamed of her behavior, so frustrated over her own weaknesses.

Blind. How horrifying that must be for a man like Ben. A physical, vibrant man. A doctor, who had skills to help and to heal. What could she do, say, to ease Ben's pain? She just didn't know.

"Oh, Ben," she whispered. "I'm so sorry this is happening to you. But you're not alone. You're not. I'm here and I—"

Megan sat bolt upward, her heart racing.

"And I…" she began, her voice trembling. "…I love you."

Dear heaven above, it was true. She was in love with Ben.

Megan got to her feet and began to pace the large room.

This was great, just dandy, she fumed. Nothing like further complicating the already tangled maze that her life, and Ben's, had become.

Love, being in love, deserved total attention and focus. It had to be nurtured, treated reverently in its newly formed, emotional state. How could she possibly do that when the hideous, ghostly presence of Charles Chastain stood ready to leap out at her at every turn?

And another thing, her mind raced on. How did Ben feel about *her?* He cared deeply for her, of that she was certain. But did he love her, even a little? Was he falling in love with her as she was with him?

Was Ben's insistence that they live in the now due to her problems and his? Or was it because he saw her with him for only the short term? Here, then gone, once the threat Charles represented had been removed.

"Hi, Ben," Megan said aloud. "How was your day? By the way, I love you. Do you love me? Want some stew?" She shook her head. "Megan, shut up."

Blind, her mind echoed. She was in love with a man who was apparently going blind. Could she deal with that? Handle it? Stand strongly by Ben's side through that kind of adversity?

Megan stopped her trek and stood still, hardly breathing as she waited for the answer, listened to the whispers from her heart, mind, her very soul.

A gentle smile formed on her lips.

For better, for worse. In sickness and in health. Until death do us part.

Yes.

This wasn't just any man—this was Ben, who had captured her heart for eternity. This was Ben, who made her want to twirl around the room in joyous wonder as she sang "You Are My Sunshine." This was Ben Rizzoli, and she would never leave him, no matter what his circumstances were.

Unless...

He sent her away.

Because he didn't love *her*.

A sudden noise from the rear of the house jerked Megan from her jumbled thoughts. A chill of fear coursed through her as she walked slowly toward the kitchen, her heart racing.

Stay calm, she told herself. The door is locked. No one can get in. Charles can't get in. No, no, he can't. The door is locked...the door—

Stop it, Megan she ordered herself as she approached the back door. *Don't fall apart now.*

She hesitated, then reached into a lower cupboard for a heavy, cast-iron skillet. With her weapon raised in her right hand, she tiptoed to the door and brushed aside the curtain with her free, shaking hand.

''Nutmeg,'' she said, hearing the thread of hysteria in her voice.

She unlocked the door and opened it. The cat strolled in, head and tail high and regal. Megan closed the door, slid the skillet onto the counter, then planted her hands on her hips.

''You gave me an awful fright, Ms. Nutmeg,'' she said. ''I suppose you're here to mooch some dinner. Well, all right. I do owe you, I guess. You were the one who made me remember that my name is Megan.'' She sighed. ''But, oh, pretty kitty, there are times when I really wish that you hadn't done that.''

Ben drove far below the speed limit as he headed for his house, postponing as much as he could the discussion he had promised to have with Megan.

He forced himself to blank his mind and savor the sight of the colorful autumn leaves on the trees edging the road leading to the house.

House, he thought suddenly. That was what it had been to him since the day it was completed and he'd moved in. His house.

Now? With Megan there waiting for him, smiling when he came through the door, hugging and kissing him in sincere welcome?

Now it was a home.

There had been laughter within those walls, and tears, serious conversations and fun. There had been lovemaking so exquisitely beautiful and meaningful that it defied description. There had been life, full and rich and wonderful.

All because Megan was there.

Ben parked in the driveway and leaned forward to fold his arms on top of the steering wheel. He swept his gaze over the majestic pine trees surrounding the house, the mountains in the distance, the first streaks of the glorious sunset being painted across the heavens by nature's magical brush.

Remember this, he told himself. *Remember every detail because the day will come when you won't be able to see it.* All he would have would be the memories as he lived out his life in darkness.

And he'd remember, too, what it had been like, how fantastic, to come *home* to Megan.

With a sigh and a shake of his head, Ben got out of the vehicle and crossed the yard to the front door of the house. When he entered the living room, he closed the door behind him, then stopped dead in his tracks, his heart beating so wildly he could feel the painful cadence of it hammering in his chest.

Soft music was playing on the stereo and Megan halted in mid-sway to smile at him. Nutmeg was cradled in her arms, like a baby.

Waning sunlight poured through the glass wall, cascading over the pair like a rosy-colored waterfall. Megan's big, expressive blue eyes were sparkling like sapphires, her cheeks were flushed a pretty pink, and her smile was warm and real.

"Welcome home, Ben," she said rather breathlessly. "We have company. Nutmeg and I were dancing. I missed you."

In that moment, as he drank in the marvelous sight of Megan Chastain smiling at him, he knew that he was deeply and irrevocably in love with her.

Ben attempted to return Megan's greeting, only to realize that his throat was tight with emotion, rendering him unable to speak.

He closed the distance between them, framed her face in his hands and visually traced each of her beautiful, delicate features.

Then he lowered his head and kissed her…softly, reverently, gently and tenderly, his heart, mind and soul filled with immeasurable awe, wonder…and love.

When he raised his head, Ben looked directly into Megan's eyes.

"It's good to be *home*," he said, his voice gritty. "It's been a long day. I missed you, too, Megan."

Heated desire thrummed low within Megan, causing the flush of her cheeks to deepen.

"Oh," was all she managed to say.

Nutmeg wiggled in her arms, having apparently decided that if the dance was over, it was time to leave.

The sensuous spell was broken as Ben stepped back to allow the cat to leap to the floor and scamper toward the back door. Megan went to the stereo and turned it off. Silence fell over the room.

"Are you hungry, Ben?" she said, a thread of breathlessness in her voice. "Dinner is ready."

Ben nodded. "I'll wash up and we'll eat. Then we have to talk, Megan."

"Yes," she said quietly. "I know."

Neither moved. They were a room apart, but the weaving, crackling sensuality wove around and through them, making it seem as though they were close, nestled against each other. Wanting. Needing. Heated passion consuming them.

Ben spun on his heel and strode from the room.

Megan pressed one hand over her racing heart and drew a shuddering breath.

"Gracious," she whispered, then started toward the kitchen.

She stopped and looked back at the empty place where Ben had stood.

She had just been kissed by the man she loved, she thought. The memory of that kiss would be tucked in the treasure chest in her heart for eternity, to be cherished, relived, in the future.

Future, her mind repeated. What did it hold for her and Ben? She didn't know. She just didn't know.

Chapter Eight

When Ben entered the kitchen, Megan was placing bowls of hot stew on the table. She'd also made a fruit salad that she'd put in a pretty lead-crystal bowl she'd found in the back of a cupboard.

"What would you like to drink with dinner?" she said, smiling at Ben. "Should I whip out the old coffee, tea or me joke?"

Ben frowned. "The back door isn't locked, Megan."

Megan glanced quickly at the door, then back at Ben.

"It was locked all day, Ben," she said. "I just forgot to redo it when I let Nutmeg in, then out again. She just went on her merry way. Do you want coffee? Iced tea? Water?"

"The doors have to be locked when I'm not here," Ben said, his frown still firmly in place. "I thought you understood that."

"You're getting a glass of water," she said, matching his expression.

Megan marched to the sink, filled two glasses with water, then returned to the table. She thunked the glasses down with such force that some water splashed into Ben's bowl of stew.

"Nice shot," he said, then sank onto his chair. "There's nothing like watered-down stew to hit the culinary spot."

"That's it." Megan planted her hands on her hips as she stood behind her chair opposite Ben. "I don't know what happened to your chipper mood between the time you greeted me, then went to wash your hands, but you'd better just knock it off, mister."

Ben stared at her with wide eyes and his mouth actually dropped open.

"I realize that you have a great deal on your mind, Ben," Megan rushed on, "and I'm sure you're not looking forward to discussing your personal nightmare. But that doesn't give you license to take it out on me by auditioning for the Grump of the Year Award. Got that?" She plopped down onto her chair. "And close your mouth. You look like a goldfish."

Ben snapped his mouth closed, shook his head and chuckled.

An angry Megan was a study in sensational, he thought. Her blue eyes were flashing like laser beams, and there was a pretty flush high on her cheeks.

Heaven help him, he loved this woman so much, so damn much.

Megan narrowed her eyes and flattened her hands on the table on either side of her silverware.

"I heard that chuckle, Dr. Rizzoli," she said. "Are you laughing at me? Are you treating me like a child who is throwing a temper tantrum? Well, I've got news for you, bub. You just better not be."

The small smile that had formed on Ben's lips when he'd chuckled disappeared.

"No, Megan," he said seriously. "I'm not laughing at you. You're absolutely right. I was taking my stress out on you and that's neither fair, nor acceptable. I apologize."

"Oh." Megan pursed her lips, then beamed in the next instant. "Well, fancy that." She laughed. "I guess I told you, huh?"

Ben reached across the table and covered one of her hands with one of his.

"You gave me hell," he said, looking directly into her eyes. "You stood up for yourself and didn't allow me to inflict…well, emotional abuse on you. Think about it, Megan. Think about how strong you've become, how much you've grown, changed, since you got out from under Chastain's shadow."

Megan nodded slowly. "You're right. I *have* changed." She sighed. "But last night I was the old Megan, who was terrified, trembling in fear of

Charles. I'm not completely free of my past, or my fears.''

"Last night was entirely my fault," Ben said, his hold on her hand tightening. "I'm very ashamed of my behavior, of what I put you through. I was feeling so damn sorry for myself.

"I'm not handling my situation well, Megan, not even close, but that's no excuse for exploding at you the way I did.''

Ben released her hand and sank back in his chair, sucking in a shuddering breath at the same time.

"I'm going to be blind at some point in the future, Megan," he said, his voice raspy. "Somehow, *somehow,* I have to learn how to accept that reality before I go right over the edge of my sanity.''

"How do you know that you're going to be blind?" Megan said, hardly above a whisper. "I mean, do you have a disease of some kind that will cause you to…to lose your sight?''

"No, not really." Ben averted his eyes from Megan's and began to fiddle with his spoon. "It's nothing like that. They can't even find the gene that's causing this. It's frustrating and…and hopeless.

"My father went blind before he died. My oldest brother is blind. The next oldest brother is having the symptoms. Hell, for all I know he has lost his sight totally by now. I haven't talked to him since last year, didn't want to hear it. I'm just sitting around waiting for my turn.''

"I see," Megan said.

Ben's head snapped up. "Got it in one. You see. I won't."

"Ben, I didn't mean it like that."

He sighed. "I know. But that's it in a nutshell. I have no future, Megan, nothing worth talking about, nothing to offer.

"Hell, I can never even father a child in fear it would be a boy and inherit whatever this mysterious menace is. It's affecting only the male Rizzolis and—forget it, your dinner is getting cold."

"So is yours."

"I'm not very hungry. I appreciate all you did to prepare this meal, but I think I'll pass. I'm going for a walk."

"Don't…you…move," she said, pointing one finger at him.

"What?"

"You heard me, Ben Rizzoli. You can't drop all this on me, then walk out the door. You said that we'd discuss it together."

"There's nothing more to say," he said, his voice rising.

"Oh, there certainly is." Megan folded her arms over her breasts. "What's this nonsense about having no future, nothing to offer? That's ridiculous."

"Damn it, Megan, there's not a big demand out there for blind doctors." Ben got to his feet. "This discussion is closed."

"Fine," she said, glaring at him. "Run. Run and hide, Ben. Run, just like I did that day in the woods before I fell, before you found me. It solves nothing, because there's nowhere to hide from truths like yours, like mine. Facts are facts.

"Ben, you keep telling me to decide what *I'm* going to do. Keep silent, or expose the real Charles Chastain to the public's view. I don't yet know what I'll do because I'm not certain how strong I've become.

"But one thing is very firm in my mind. I will no longer run. When Charles finds me—and he will—*I will not run and hide from him.* When are *you* going to stop running, Ben?"

A muscle ticked in Ben's tightly clenched jaw, then he strode to the back door and left the house, slamming the door behind him.

Megan cringed as the window in the door rattled from the impact. She propped her elbow on the table and rested her chin on her palm.

That had definitely not gone well, she thought miserably. She had thoroughly blown it. Of all the ways she might have reacted to what Ben had finally shared with her, bared his soul about, she'd obviously chosen the wrong one.

In all fairness to herself, she had no experience in reaching out to someone of importance to her. During her years with Charles, she'd been centered on herself, just trying to survive each day as it came.

She needed to remember that, be patient with herself as well as with Ben, because darn it, she loved him, and refused to give up on him. He was standing by her side as she dealt with her problems, and she'd do the same for him, whether he liked it or not.

I have no future, Megan, nothing worth talking about, nothing to offer. I can never even father a child...a child...a child....

Loving Ben, having a future with Ben, meant she'd never have his baby. How did she feel about that? She wanted a child so very much and—

Megan Chastain, she mentally admonished, *listen to yourself.* She was doing it again. She was focusing on herself, turning things inward, instead of reaching out to Ben, who was in such pain, suffering through such heartache and fear.

She had a great deal to learn about being a woman in love, needed to move beyond the person she had been in the past, so she could be all she should be for Ben.

Aren't you forgetting something? a little voice in her mind nagged. Oh, yes, she certainly was.

She had no idea if Ben Rizzoli loved her.

"Oh, drat," she said, getting to her feet. "Everything is so complicated. There's definitely something to be said for having amnesia."

Megan picked up the two glasses of water from the table and started toward the sink. Just as she passed the back door, it burst open.

In one tick of time, Megan screamed, spun around, and flung the contents of the glasses in the direction of the noise.

One dose hit Ben squarely in the face, the other splattered against his chest.

"Ben!" Megan said, holding the empty glasses

straight out in front of her. "What...what are you doing here?"

Ben dragged one hand down his dripping face, then pulled his soggy shirt away from his chest with his thumb and forefinger.

"For one thing," he said, blinking water from his eyes, "I live here. For another, I realized that if I went storming off in the dark like a three-year-old in a snit, I'd probably end up thunking my head on a tree, or whatever."

"Oh." Megan put the glasses on the counter and rushed to Ben. She fluttered her hands in the air as she reached toward his wet shirt, then changed her mind. "Oh, dear. Oh, dear."

"Well," Ben said, a slow smile creeping onto his lips, "bring on Chastain. I don't have to worry about you. You'll just drown the creep."

It was too much, it really was. Within a very few minutes the atmosphere in the house had changed from intense to definitely silly.

Megan fell apart.

She laughed so hard, she had to wrap her arms around her stomach and gulp for air. Every time she looked at soggy Ben, it set her off again. She leaned against the counter and laughed until tears of merriment spilled onto her cheeks.

The sound was infectious, and Ben made no attempt to curb the broad smile that broke across his face.

Oh, yeah, he thought, this was his Megan, and this

was just one of the ways that she transformed this house into a home.

Her laughter was like beautiful wind chimes, clear, pure and real. The sound was dancing through the air, chasing away the gloom…and the darkness.

Her mother had been so very right all those years ago…Megan was sunshine.

And he loved her.

"My, my, my," Megan said finally, placing one hand on her heart. "What a hoot."

She dashed the tears from her cheeks and smiled at Ben. "Hey, look at the bright side. We could have had soda with dinner, complete with ice cubes."

Another bubble of laughter escaped from her lips. "Picture that. No, don't. If I laugh any more, I'll get the hiccups for sure."

"You're finished then?" Ben said, grinning at her.

"I certainly hope so. I'm running out of oxygen." Megan took a deep breath and let it out slowly. "There. All done. I'm fine. I should apologize, I suppose, for drenching you, but you *did* scare the bejeebers out of me, you know."

"No apology is necessary," Ben said, beginning to unbutton his shirt. "I acted like a jerk. You're right, Megan. It's time that I stopped running. I'm overdue to square off and face reality as it stands. It took you, what you said tonight, plus what you've done in regard to *your* reality to make me see that." He paused. "Thank you."

"You said that I wasn't alone in dealing with Charles, or my past," Megan said seriously. "You're not alone, either. I'm here for you, Ben.'' And I love you so much, Ben Rizzoli. "I'm here.''

"Yeah, well...'' Ben stopped speaking and pulled his shirt free of his pants.

"Would you care for a bowl of reheated stew, Dr. Rizzoli?'' Megan said.

"That sounds great,'' he said. "I'll go change and be right back. I'll wipe up the water from the floor after we eat. It's the least I can do.''

"Indeed,'' Megan said with a burst of laughter. She flapped one hand in front of her face. "No, no, I'm not going to start *that* again.'' She cleared her throat. "Okay. I'm under control.''

"Nuke the stew,'' Ben said, chuckling. "I shall return, ma'am.''

Ben strode from the room and Megan's smile faded as she watched him go.

Blind, she thought. Life was so unfair at times. Why was such a horrendous thing happening to a wonderful man like Ben? Well, that was one question that would never have an answer.

And the multitude of other questions and unknowns?

Megan sighed and picked up the bowls of cold stew from the table.

The answers would come, one at a time, she supposed, as she and Ben inched their way into the future. Together. For now.

But she wished she knew if Ben Rizzoli loved her.

Much later, Megan sat on the sofa in front of a crackling fire in the hearth, snuggled close to Ben, her legs tucked up beside her. He had quietly explained the extensive research his friend, Dr. Fred Bolstad, was conducting on behalf of the male Rizzolis.

He also told her that Fred had urged him to contact his brothers for an update on the condition of their eyes, since it had been many months since Ben had done so.

"Why are you hesitating to do that?" Megan said, her head nestled on Ben's shoulder.

"Two reasons," he said. "One…I honestly didn't want to hear what they had to say. It's the old head-in-the-sand bit. If you don't tell me, I don't have to deal with *my* truth."

Ben shook his head in self-disgust. "My level of maturity is seriously lacking something at times."

"And the second reason?" Megan said.

"My siblings are like strangers to me, Megan. I don't really know them. Four of them were grown and out of the house before I was born.

"They came to visit our folks on various holidays, but quick trips didn't cement any kind of bond between us. For all practical purposes, I'm an only child. My last two brothers were gone from home before I started kindergarten."

"That's rather sad," Megan said. "You know, to have a large family but…well, to not really have one."

Ben lifted one shoulder in a shrug. "That's just the way it is. Anyway, I don't feel that comfortable

intruding in my brothers' lives, forcing them to discuss something that I know for a fact is very painful
and upsetting. Do you understand where I'm coming
from?''

"Yes. Yes, I do."

"Two of my brothers have sons. Can you imagine
what it's like for them to look at those little boys
and—cripes. At least that's one thing I won't have
to deal with. I'll never have children. Never.''

"Yes,'' Megan said slowly. "I understand that,
too. It was a rather stark statement when you first
made it, but it's the only sensible thing to do. Well,
there are a multitude of children out there who need
a home, a family, love. You could adopt children.''

"Yeah, right. I'm sure an agency would be thrilled
to hand over a kid to a blind man. Not a chance.''

"Let's not get into that right now,'' Megan said.
"But you should contact your brothers like Fred Bolstad asked you to.''

Ben sighed. "I will. Soon.'' He paused. "I hate to
break up the party, but I forgot to do something.''
He eased Megan away from him and got to his feet.

"What did you forget to do?'' she said, looking
up at him questioningly.

"When I came barreling in to have my water glass
shower,'' he said, frowning, "I forgot to lock the
back door.''

"Oh,'' Megan said quietly.

Back to reality, she thought dismally.

The next morning while Megan and Ben were having breakfast the telephone rang.

"Uh-oh, Dr. Rizzoli," Megan said. "I bet someone has a problem that needs your attention."

"Yep," Ben said, getting to his feet.

He crossed the room and snatched up the receiver mounted on the wall.

"Hello?"

"Ben? Hi, it's Andrea."

"Good morning," he said.

"Listen, the woman who manages the Sleeping Beauty shop here in the hotel has the flu, and her backup is out of town. I could cover the store, but I thought Megan might be getting cabin fever, being cooped up at your place day after day. I've worked at Sleeping Beauty in the past and it's fun. Would Megan like to do it today?"

Ben frowned. "Hang on a minute."

"Sure."

Ben covered the mouthpiece with one hand and related to Megan what Andrea had said.

"Oh, yes," Megan said. "I'd love to. Oh, dear, I only have jeans and my one pretty dress. Well, the dress ought to be suitable."

"Whoa," Ben said. "I can understand why you'd like to get out of here for a day, but if you're going to be that out in the open, that exposed, I want to fill Brandon and Andrea in on what's going on with Chastain so they can keep an eye on things. Especially Brandon."

"Oh." Megan's bright smile changed into a frown. "We'd have to tell them the whole ugly story, wouldn't we?"

Ben nodded.

"Well, all right," Megan said slowly. "Yes, that's fine. I consider them to be some of the new friends I've made here in Prescott, friends who will be there for me in good times *and* bad. Don't you think that's true?"

"You bet," Ben said. "Andrea, Brandon, the aunts, Jennifer, are all there for you if you need them."

"And for you, too, Ben. They've been close to you since you were a little boy. Don't you believe you should share *your* problem with all of them?"

"This isn't the time to discuss *that*," he said, glaring at her. He placed the receiver back against his ear. "Andrea? Megan would be happy to take over Sleeping Beauty today. We'll hustle up here and come into town, because we need to meet with you and Brandon and discuss something before I have to get to the office."

"Okay," Andrea said. "We'll be waiting for you two. See you soon, and tell Megan thank you for doing this on such short notice."

"Well, thanks for thinking of her."

"Of course I thought of her, Ben. She's one of the family now—our friend. 'Bye."

Ben replaced the receiver, then ran a hand over the back of his neck.

"You're one of the family now, to quote Andrea," he said. "As well as a friend."

"That's lovely," Megan said quietly.

Ben returned to the table and sat opposite Megan.

"We'll have to get going here," he said.

"Ben—"

"Megan, don't push," he said, meeting her gaze. "Yes, I realize I have close friends here, but... Hell, I don't want their pity, don't want to see it in their eyes, on their faces, hear them express endless sympathy about what is going to happen to me."

"Why not?" Megan said, leaning toward him. "Those are all different kinds of hugs. Everyone needs hugs when they're in trouble. You're using the word pity in a very negative way. Erase pity. Consider their potential reactions as sincere sorrow, caring, love and concern for a dear, dear friend."

"No," Ben said, then drained his coffee mug. "Go put on your pretty dress."

Megan got to her feet. "You are so stubborn, Rizzoli. If I was Andrea, Brandon, or one of the others, I'd be very hurt that you didn't trust me enough to come to me with what you're facing.

"Do you want them to believe that you're only a fair-weather friend? That they're not to count on you during *their* difficult times? After all, you didn't confide in them during yours. Think about it."

Megan stuck her nose in the air and marched from the room.

"Women," Ben muttered. "Their busy, complicated minds never stop, just operate on high-octane twenty-four hours a day." He sank back in his chair and sighed. "Great. That's all I needed. Something else to think about."

* * *

"There you have it," Ben said to Andrea and Brandon a short time later. "Just stay on alert, Brandon. Cable Montana agrees with me that Chastain probably has a detective, if not more than one, looking for Megan. Be aware of anyone who might hang around Sleeping Beauty too long today."

"Got it," Brandon said.

The four were in the large conference room off the lobby of Hamilton House where they could speak in private.

"I'm terribly sorry about what you've been through, Megan," Andrea said.

Here it comes, Ben thought. The pity, the oh-poor-you junk. Megan might consider that garbage as welcomed hugs, but he'd pass, thank you very much.

"But that's all behind you now," Andrea said brightly. "It's onward and upward, looking to the future." She laughed. "At the risk of sounding like Aunt Charity, I think you should kick Charles Chastain's butt."

Brandon chuckled. "You definitely sound like Aunt Charity, my sweet."

"Well, Charles Chastain shouldn't be allowed to go merrily on his way," Andrea said. "Good heavens, Brandon, that man wants to be governor of our state. No way. Nope. Not a chance."

That was it? Ben thought incredulously. One little "I'm terribly sorry, Megan," then onward and upward? Unbelievable.

"I'm still sorting through my options," Megan said, bringing Ben back to attention.

"Well, we're here for you," Andrea said, "no matter what you decide to do. Come on, I'll show you how to operate the fancy cash register that Janice has in Sleeping Beauty. Oh, Janice and Taylor will be coming up here tomorrow for Joey's birthday party. 'Bye, Ben. Go play doctor with someone.''

Megan smiled warmly at Ben, then the two women left the room, laughing and talking. Brandon frowned and shook his head.

"How many minutes would you like to have alone with Chastain, Ben?" he said.

"Ten," Ben said gruffly.

"Me, too. I can't stomach guys who beat up on women. Man, Chastain is lower than low. He has to be exposed, the truth told about him.''

"That's Megan's call, Brandon.''

"Yeah, I suppose." Brandon paused. "Megan seems relaxed and happy. Considering what she's been through with Chastain, not to mention her case of amnesia, that's pretty remarkable.''

"She's an incredible woman, and she's a lot stronger than she even realizes," Ben said. "Megan is intelligent, too, and...fun, you know what I mean? And when she laughs? Hell, the whole house— home—is filled with sunshine. That's not to say she doesn't have a temper. She can get in a rip that—" He stopped talking and frowned. "What are you grinning like a fool about, Hamilton?''

"Welcome to the love club, buddy," Brandon said, punching Ben on the arm. "You're down for the count. Does Megan know that you're in love with her?''

Ben opened his mouth to deny the claim that Brandon was making, then decided it wouldn't do any good. Brandon Hamilton had known him too well, for too long.

"No," Ben said quietly. "She has no idea how I feel about her. Well, she knows that I care deeply for her, but..." He shrugged.

"So? Tell her you're in love with her."

"No," Ben said. "There's no purpose to be served by doing that."

"You've lost me here, Rizzoli. Megan is free to do as she pleases. If she's in love with you—well, hell, man, you can have the whole enchilada. A wife, kids, a home, a future with the woman you love. What do you mean, there's no purpose to be served by telling her that you're in love with her? That should be the first thing on your agenda."

"I said no, Brandon, so drop it, would you? I'm outta here. I have patients to see."

"Hold it," Brandon said. "There has been something heavy on your mind for many months, Ben. We've all been aware of that, all of us who care about you.

"I think whatever is wrong is keeping you from going after what you could have with Megan. What is it? Come on, buddy, this is me, Brandon." He splayed one hand on his chest. "Talk to me."

With a muscle ticking in his tightly clenched jaw, Ben stared at his lifelong friend for several moments. Then he spun on his heel and strode from the room.

Chapter Nine

After Megan had rung up two sales on the rather complicated cash register in Sleeping Beauty without mishap, she relaxed and soon realized she was thoroughly enjoying herself.

The women who wandered into the shop were pleasant and friendly—obviously in a laid-back vacation frame of mind. There was none of the hustle and bustle and please-hurry-dear attitude that Megan was accustomed to while shopping in Phoenix.

Janice's merchandise, Megan decided early on, was scrumptious, so feminine and luscious.

She straightened and folded silk and satin teddies, camisoles, tap pants and nightgowns. There were scented candles with matching fragrances in bath beads, crystals and soaps. A woman would feel pretty, pampered and feminine with any purchase made at Sleeping Beauty.

At noon, Andrea appeared at the shop with a glass of iced tea and a sandwich, which Megan ate while sitting on the high stool behind the counter. Andrea expressed the desire to join Megan for the meal, but she had a business luncheon with a new client of her advertising firm.

In the middle of the afternoon, Megan wrapped a purchase in pretty paper for a customer to give as a birthday gift, causing Megan to remember that she didn't have a present to take to Joey's birthday party the next day.

She called Ben's office and asked the woman who answered the telephone to please have Ben phone her at the shop when he had a free moment. Fifteen minutes later, the telephone on the end of the counter rang.

"Sleeping Beauty," Megan answered cheerfully.

"That's convenient," Ben said, "because this is Prince Charming. Wake up."

Megan laughed. "That's not how the story goes. You're supposed to kiss me awake."

Ben made a loud smacking kiss. "How's that?"

"Needs practice," she said, still smiling.

"Mmm. That can be arranged. How's it going there? Having fun?"

"Oh, my, yes," she said. "I really am."

"Good. What can I do for you, ma'am? I'm returning your call, you know."

"I wondered if you'd mind going shopping when

you pick me up this evening. I need to buy a present for Joey.''

''So do I. It was on my list of things to do, but I lost the list.'' Ben paused. ''We could grab a hamburger, then hit the toy store.''

''I have no idea what a five-year-old boy would like.''

''I do. I was a five-year-old boy a million years ago. If it has lots of moving parts and makes noise, we're in business.''

Megan frowned. ''Oh, dear. I got caught up in the idea of Joey's gift and just remembered I don't have any money to buy it.''

''No problem. We'll get something great and put both our names on the card. Gotta go. See you later.''

''''Bye, Ben.''

Megan replaced the receiver slowly. She sighed, then frowned.

She was in limbo, she thought. She was free of Charles, but yet, she wasn't. She had no money, none of her clothes or personal possessions, no way to be truly independent.

Megan propped her elbow on the counter and rested her chin in her palm.

She was waiting for Charles to find her, was convinced that he would eventually manage to do that. There would be an ugly confrontation of some sort, and then somewhere down the road she'd *really* be free.

Megan straightened, her frown deepening.

This was dumb. Why was she putting her life on hold until Charles located her?

"That's easy enough to answer," she said aloud.

Because she was terrified of the man, was postponing that final scene as long as possible, like a frightened child. There was also the fact that she hadn't yet determined if she was going to go public with the truth about Charles Chastain.

This was getting ridiculous. She was mooching off Ben just as Nutmeg the cat did. How long did she expect Ben to feed and clothe her, keep a roof over her head?

It was time to gather more courage, reach deeper within herself for the strength to be proactive. She would inform her attorney as to her whereabouts and have him tell Charles that she planned to make one trip to the enormous house in Phoenix to collect her belongings.

A shiver of fear coursed through Megan as she envisioned herself walking through the front door of that house. The house of terror she could only pray would fade from her memory in time.

Think about the future, she ordered herself, not the past. Think about Ben, not Charles. Think about sunshine and happiness beyond measure, not evil darkness and disillusionment.

Tonight. Yes, tonight she'd telephone her attorney at his home and make arrangements for him to escort her to the house she'd shared with Charles Chastain. She'd claim what was rightfully hers and then...

"Then...what?" she said.

She didn't know.

Because she had no idea if Ben Rizzoli loved her, wanted her to stay by his side, continue to live with him.

Ben saw himself as a man with no future, nothing to offer, because of the horrible shadow of his pending blindness that hovered over him. Even if he loved her, would he send her away because of what he was facing?

Megan pressed her fingertips to her temples.

There were still so many unanswered questions, so many unknowns, so much to deal with. It was all such a complicated, tangled maze.

Megan was pulled from her thoughts by a man entering the shop. She slid off the stool and moved to the front of the counter.

"May I help you find something?" she said, smiling.

The burly man, who wore a dark suit, white shirt and dark tie, did not return her smile.

"No, I've found what I was looking for," he said. "Mrs. Chastain."

Megan felt the color drain from her face and her knees begin to tremble.

"What…what do you want?" she said, hearing the quivering in her voice.

"It's very simple," the man said. "You just come with me. Quietly. No fuss. We walk out of here, and Mr. Chastain will forget that this little escapade of yours ever took place. You've had your fun, but the show is over. Let's go. You're expected in Phoenix."

Megan took a step backward. "No. I'm not going anywhere with you. You have three seconds to leave this shop, or I'll scream the roof down."

"No, I don't think you will," the man said, his voice low and menacing. "You see, Mrs. Chastain, you've been ill, emotionally unstable. Mr. Chastain has documents prepared citing numerous events that have taken place that indicate you need to be committed to an institution for professional care."

"You're crazy," Megan whispered.

"No, you are. Let's see here. You tried to burn the house down. You came at Mr. Chastain with a butcher knife. What else? Oh, you almost made it out the front door stark naked.

"And now? You ran away to be with your lover in this hick town. You're a sick cookie, Mrs. Chastain, but your concerned ex-husband will have you put away to recover, as he struggles against his tears of heartache when he makes the announcement to the press."

"Lies. It's all lies."

"Of course it is, but who will believe *you,* when Charles Chastain is the one telling them? If you don't come with me now, your next stop is a long stretch at the funny farm."

"Charles will never get away with this," Megan said, taking another step backward.

"Yes, he will, and you know it. Oh, and Mrs. Chastain? In case you're on the fence about your decision, Mr. Chastain wishes you to know that charges will be filed against Dr. Benjamin Rizzoli."

"What?" Megan said, her eyes widening.

"As a medical man, the good doctor realized you were unbalanced. He took advantage of you, seduced you, was after the Chastain money. Rizzoli will beat that rap, but his credibility as a doctor will be so questioned in the interim that he can kiss his practice goodbye. His reputation will be shot to hell."

"No, oh, no. Please. Don't hurt, Ben," Megan said, her eyes filling with tears. "Don't do this."

"It's up to you, Mrs. Chastain." The man paused. "Ready to go? My car is parked across the street. You'll be back in Mr. Chastain's arms in a couple of hours and your little trip up here will be forgiven."

"I...I have to think," Megan said, shaking her head. "I...I need time to think. I—"

"There's nothing to think about," the man said. "You're coming with me—now."

A large hand clamped down on one of the man's shoulders.

"Oh, that's just not possible," Brandon said. "Megan has to run this store. She can't leave it unattended. Hit the road, chum."

The man shrugged off Brandon's hand and turned to face him.

"Don't get involved, sucker," he said. "You'll be in way over your head."

"Really?" Brandon said, raising his eyebrows. "That's not how I see it...sucker. This isn't Chastain's turf. He should have mentioned that before he sent you up here."

Ben ran in the front door of the hotel with Cable Montana right behind him. Moments later, both men were in Sleeping Beauty. Andrea nodded in satisfaction from behind the registration desk and started across the lobby to join the group.

"Megan?" Ben went to her and pulled her close, holding her tightly.

"Oh, Ben," she said, tears shimmering in her eyes and echoing in her voice as she looked up at him. "You mustn't do this, because Charles is going to destroy you. He is, Ben. He is."

"Not in this lifetime, sweetheart," Ben said, then dropped a quick kiss on her lips.

Ben released Megan, set her away from him gently, then stepped in front of the man.

"Walk out, or be carried," Ben said, a steely edge to his voice.

"Vote for carried," Brandon said, close to the man's ear. "Come on, be a sport."

"Hold it," Cable Montana said, moving between Ben and the man.

"He hasn't voted yet, Cable," Brandon said.

"Brandon, hush," Andrea said, unable to curb her smile.

Cable pushed his Stetson up with one thumb and looked directly into the man's eyes.

"Here's the story," the sheriff said. "I can arrest you for attempting to intimidate a woman on a Friday, wearing a tie past noon within the city limits, and having an unattended flat tire. Or you can leave."

"You're nuts," the man said. "Those aren't laws."

"In Prescott they are," Cable said, smiling.

"And I don't have a damn flat tire," the man said, none too quietly.

"Yes," Cable said, nodding. "You do. It's in the front, right by the vanity plate that says Chastain 4. Noticed it when I was coming in here. Sometimes it just doesn't pay to advertise."

"You're going to regret this," the man said, sweeping his gaze wildly over the entire group. "Big time." He pushed his way past Brandon, left the store and hurried across the lobby toward the front door.

"Wearing a tie past noon?" Brandon said, chuckling as he looked at Cable.

"I thought that was a nice touch," Cable said, lifting one shoulder in a shrug. "Wasn't bad, considering I was winging it. Thanks for the phone call, Andrea."

"My pleasure," Andrea said. "I punched in those numbers to call you and Ben so fast, I nearly broke my finger. But everything worked out just fine, didn't it?"

"No, it didn't," Brandon said. "Ben didn't get to deck the creep."

"Stop it," Megan said, tears streaking down her cheeks. "You're all acting as though this is a game, a joke. You didn't hear what that man said, what Charles intends to do. To me. To Ben. And he will. He can. Don't any of you understand that? Don't you realize who you're dealing with? You've got to listen to me. Please. You must—''

"Hey, whoa," Ben said, pulling Megan into his arms again. "Take it easy."

"What exactly did that thug say?" Cable said. "What messages did he deliver to you from Chastain?"

"Give it a rest, Montana," Ben said, glaring at the sheriff. "Can't you see that Megan's been through enough for one day?"

"I want to fully document what happened here today, Ben," Cable said. "I can't do anything with it at this point because Chastain would deny everything, say the guy was acting on his own, or that Megan fabricated the whole thing. But to be on the safe side, I intend to have this episode on record."

"That makes sense," Andrea said. "But why don't we close the store and move into the conference room? We're drawing a crowd in the lobby, and heaven only knows what stories will circulate about what happened in here."

Cable nodded. "You're right. Okay, keep it simple. Megan was upset by a man who tried to make a move on her and who became very insistent." He shrugged. "We sent him on his way."

"Got it, Brandon said.

"Fine," Andrea said. "Let's go where we can speak privately."

"No," Ben said. "I'll call my office and have the rest of my appointments rescheduled. I'm taking Megan home. Now."

"Ben, look..." Cable started.

"Hello?" Megan said, moving out of Ben's embrace. "Remember me? I have a voice, you know, an opinion. Granted, I fell apart when that...that creature threatened Ben, but up until then I was holding my own." She frowned. "Well, sort of. I'll give you the information you want, Sheriff Montana...Cable."

"You don't have to do this," Ben said.

"Yes, I do, Ben," she said, looking directly at him. "What just happened has shown me that I have a long way to go to be able to stand up to Charles, to be strong enough. Messages from him intimidate me, for heaven's sake. Let me salvage at least a modicum of my pride here."

Ben threw up his hands in defeat.

"Thank you, Megan," Cable said. "This shouldn't take long."

"I need to go cover the registration desk," Andrea said. "I'll call your office for you, Ben, and say you won't be back today."

Megan, Ben, Cable, and Brandon crossed the lobby, went into the conference room and closed the door. Megan sank onto one of the chairs.

"Take your time, Megan," Cable said gently.

"Charles..." Megan began, then cleared her throat and lifted her chin. Her hands were clutched tightly in her lap. "Charles has put together false documentation of incidents that show that I'm mentally unbalanced.

"According to him, I have attempted to burn down

the house. I've come at him with a butcher knife.
I'm completely nuts. If I don't return to him, he'll
have me committed to an institution.''

"That cooks it," Ben said, starting toward the
door. "It's time I paid a visit to Chastain."

Cable moved quickly, grabbing one of Ben's arms.

"Hold it right there," the sheriff said. "I told you
before that all that would get you was a stretch in
jail for assault.''

Ben narrowed his eyes. "Get your hand off me,
Montana. I can deal with an assault charge. It'll be
worth it to have ten minutes alone with Chastain."

"No!" Megan jumped to her feet. "You'd be
playing right into his hands, Ben. He plans to file
charges against you already, saying that you took advantage of me, seduced me. That you were after the
Chastain money.''

"What?" Ben said.

"He'd never make that stick," Cable said, releasing Ben's arm.

"Charles knows that," Megan said. "But it would
raise questions, cast enough doubt on Ben's reputation that his medical practice might very well be de-
stroyed. It was when I heard that...well, I...I just
lost it.''

Ben took a deep breath and let it out slowly. "That
man," he said, a raw edge to his voice, "has got to
be stopped.''

"I agree," Cable said. "But beating him to a pulp
isn't the way to do it. You're a doctor, Ben. You

heal people, put them back together. You don't take them apart.''

"Well, damn," Brandon said. "That makes sense. I wish it didn't, but it does. I'm all for Ben popping Chastain in the chops, but it's not the road to go."

"Nope," Cable said. "There's only one way that Chastain can be cut off at the knees."

"And that's by making a public announcement, backed up by medical reports, that Charles Chastain is a wife beater," Megan said quietly.

"Yes, ma'am," Cable said, tugging his Stetson low on his forehead, shadowing his eyes. "But that decision is entirely yours to make. I'll catch you folks later."

Cable strode from the room, then Brandon gave Megan a quick hug and followed the sheriff out the door.

"Ben," Megan said. "Promise me you won't confront Charles. Please? I have so much to deal with that I can't be worrying about that, too. Promise me."

Ben sighed and shook his head. "Yeah, all right, I promise. I don't like it, but...okay."

"And you have enough to deal with regarding your personal situation without having to worry about me. I need to put distance between us, Ben. I'm bringing nothing but threats and grief into your life."

Ben closed the distance between them and framed Megan's face in his hands.

"Wrong," he said. "You're forgetting a long list

of other very important things you've added to my existence, one of which is front row center in my mind at the moment.''

''Which one?''

Ben smiled. ''Sunshine. And, ah, Megan, as dark as my future is going to be, that is a precious, precious gift I will always cherish.''

Ben lowered his head and kissed Megan, softly, gently, brushing his lips over hers. Then he returned to capture her mouth in a searing kiss that caused the smoldering embers of desire within them to burst into licking flames that consumed them.

The kiss pushed into oblivion the cold fear of what had taken place in Sleeping Beauty, replacing it with the heat of passion, intertwined with the soothing warmth of caring.

Ben raised his head and took a sharp breath. ''Not the place.''

''Conference rooms are nice,'' Megan said dreamily. She blinked. ''Oh. Goodness. Shame on me.''

Ben chuckled. ''Come on. I'll take you home.''

''No.''

''No?'' he said, raising his eyebrows.

''No,'' she repeated. ''We have a birthday present to buy for a special little boy, remember? Oh, and I want my hamburger, too.'' Megan started toward the door, glancing back at Ben over one shoulder. ''And French fries.''

Ben laughed and started after her.

Man, oh, man, he thought, how he loved that woman.

* * *

By unspoken agreement no reference was made to the incident in Sleeping Beauty while Megan and Ben consumed hamburgers, fries and thick chocolate milk shakes.

The next stop was a toy store in the mall, where Ben rubbed his hands together as he swept his gaze over the vast array.

"Oh-h-h, yeah," he said, smiling. "This is great, really great."

Megan laughed in delight. "Who is the little boy? You, or Joey?"

"My dear Megan," he said in mock seriousness, "there are certain things in life that are ageless. I'm pleased to have the opportunity to enlighten you regarding such an important matter."

"Do tell."

"I just did." Ben dropped a kiss on her lips. "Let's go check out the trucks. Trucks are good. A guy can never have too many trucks, you know what I mean? Red trucks, blue trucks—hey, one of every color. Trucks are—"

"Rizzoli?"

"Hmm?"

"Put a cork in it."

"Right."

They bought a truck.

It was over two-feet long, bright orange with oversize tires, and made a terrific whirring noise when shoved along the floor.

Once the batteries were in place, a push of a button

caused the rear section to lift and dump real, or imag-
ined, cargo, and the headlights to blink red, then
white, in a continuous rhythm.

"Now this," Ben said, holding the purchase out
at arm's length when they returned home, "is a
truck."

"It certainly is," Megan said. "How does one go
about wrapping such a thing? All those different
edges are going to poke through the paper."

"No problem, my sweet," Ben said, setting the
truck on the sofa. "We stick it in a grocery bag and
plop a bow on it. Trust me…Joey Mackane won't
give a hoot about the wrapping paper, or lack of
same. He's all boy. He'll dive right in to get to the
good stuff."

"You really like Joey, don't you?" Megan said
quietly.

"He is one neat little kid. He's smart as a whip,
funny, loves his nifty mom, and he knows that mud
puddles were put on this earth to be splashed in. Yep,
he's something." Ben started toward the kitchen.
"I'll get a sack and a roll of tape."

Ben deserved a Joey in his life, Megan mused as
he disappeared from view. Whether he could see or
not, he would be a wonderful father. It didn't require
sight to give hugs, to tell stories, to be there to talk,
share, care. Surely an adoption agency would realize
that and—

Oh, Megan, stop it, she told herself. She was envisioning Ben and a little boy in her mind's eye. And
standing right there with them in her imaginings, just

as bold as you please, was Megan Chastain, wife of
Ben, mother of his child.

Dreams, she thought with a sigh. Hopes and
dreams. Very few of which, she'd discovered thus
far in her life, ever came true.

Chapter Ten

It was a picture-perfect day for a backyard birthday party. The sky was a brilliant blue dotted with puffs of white, fluffy clouds, and the air was crisp.

Jennifer had strung rows of big balloons across the yard from the house to the back fence, creating a rainbow-colored canopy. She'd borrowed folding chairs and tables from the supply at Hamilton House, and set them around the edge of the grass to leave plenty of room for five little boys to run and play.

Ben introduced Megan to all the people she didn't know, and she was greeted with friendly smiles and heartfelt welcomes.

Everyone piled their plates high with sandwiches made from a wide variety of cold cuts, plus several different kinds of salads. The noise level was high, the chatter nonstop. A good time was being had by all.

When the birthday boy had made a wish and blown out the five candles, and the cake and ice cream had been consumed, Joey sat on the grass and began to open his gifts.

While everyone's attention was directed toward the treasures being unwrapped, Cable Montana motioned to Ben to come to the back of the assembled group.

"How's Megan doing?" Cable said, keeping his voice low enough for only Ben to hear.

"Okay," Ben said. "But we haven't discussed what happened at Sleeping Beauty."

Cable frowned. "Don't you think you should? Just because we dealt with Chastain's messenger boy and he went back to Phoenix empty-handed doesn't mean that Chastain is going to roll over and play dead."

"I like that image of him in my mind," Ben said, smiling slightly.

Cable chuckled. "Poor choice of words, considering that I'm talking to *you,* but you get the drift. Chastain has a lot to lose—hell, everything to lose— if Megan reveals the truth about him. We haven't heard the last of him, Ben. No way. Megan needs to blow the whistle on him, and the sooner the better."

"She may never have enough courage to do that, Cable," Ben said, frowning. "I won't push her, either. It has to be her decision. Sometimes reality is just too difficult to deal with."

"Yes, but hiding your head in the sand won't make the reality go away," Cable said.

No joke, Ben thought. He still hadn't called his brothers for an update on the condition of their sight. He was a pro at burying his head in the sand. But his reality hung over his head continually, like a dark, menacing cloud.

"Remember what I told you in your office, Cable. Megan has another choice," Ben said. "She can bargain with Chastain. Trade her silence for her freedom."

"True," Cable said, nodding. "But does she really want to stand silently by and watch that scum possibly become governor? And how will she feel if she reads in the newspaper that Chastain remarried? Megan would know what that woman was suffering at the hands of that sleazeball."

"Whew," Ben said, shaking his head. "You don't pull any punches, Montana."

"I want Chastain stopped, Rizzoli. I want him to pay up," Cable said tightly. "And my hands are tied without Megan's cooperation."

"I'll tell her what you said, but I won't push her. We all have to deal with…with things in our own way, in our own comfort zone."

"Or not deal with them at all?" Cable said, looking directly at Ben.

"Meaning?" Ben said, narrowing his eyes as he met the sheriff's intense gaze.

"Just what I said before. Hiding your head in the sand isn't going to cut it." Cable paused. "I get the feeling that we're discussing more than just Megan's situation here, Ben.''

"You've been a cop too long. You have a suspicious mind, buddy.'' Ben switched his gaze to Joey. "I'm going to move closer. Joey is about to unwrap the truck that Megan and I got him. If I'm lucky, he'll let me play with him and that spiffy vehicle. See you later.''

"Mmm.'' Cable watched Ben walk away. "What's your head in the sand about, Rizzoli?'' he said under his breath.

"Well, double darn it,'' Aunt Charity said. "That's what I get for taking a nap like a silly old woman. I missed the good stuff. I would have given that fella what for, by golly, for pestering you, Megan. When a lady says no to a man's advances, the answer is no.'' She nodded. "I would have made that clear, by gum.''

"Calm down, dear,'' Aunt Prudence said, patting her twin sister on the knee. "Ben, Brandon and Cable took care of the situation in short order. Let's change the subject, shall we?''

Bless you, Aunt Prudence, Megan thought. She didn't want to dwell on what had happened in Sleeping Beauty. Not now. Not on Joey's birthday.

"Oh,'' Andrea said, her eyes widening as she splayed both hands on her stomach. "Baby Hamilton is doing an Olympic-form tumbling act. I think I overdid the sugary cake and ice cream.''

Janice Sinclair smiled. "Being pregnant has made you glow, Andrea."

Andrea laughed. "I don't glow when I have to get up three or four times in the night to go to the bathroom. I'm definitely grumpy."

The women sitting in the circle of chairs laughed. Megan swept her gaze over the aunts, Andrea and Janice.

Janice Sinclair was so beautiful, Megan thought, yet she gave the impression that it was of little importance to her. She had gorgeous blond hair, big blue eyes and a stunning figure. The breeze had tousled her hair, and she hadn't bothered to reapply her lipstick after eating lunch. She was just...Janice, and Megan had liked her from the moment they'd been introduced.

In fact, she was fond of so many people here in Prescott. She wanted to stay in this enchanting little town, start over here, surrounded by such warm, friendly, loving people...family.

Most of all, she wanted to stay with Ben.

"I appreciate it, Megan," Janice said, pulling Megan from her thoughts.

"Pardon me?" Megan said. "I...I drifted off somewhere."

"I was saying thank you for stepping in and running Sleeping Beauty yesterday," Janice said. "I'm just sorry you had the nasty experience with that man." Janice paused and looked at Andrea. "I think perhaps I should have a larger standby staff available for the shop."

Andrea nodded. "I believe you're right. People take vacations, get the flu, and what have you. There's an endless number of retired women in Prescott who might be happy to have a workday now and then. It would break their routine, and also give them some personal pin money, as the old saying goes."

"That's not an old saying," Aunt Charity said. "I use that phrase all the time, and I'm not completely decrepit, just because I take an afternoon nap once in a while."

"Every afternoon, dear," Aunt Prudence said pleasantly. "If we don't, we nod off during the ten o'clock news and don't hear the weather report."

"That is no one's business, Prudence," Charity said with an indignant sniff.

"Charity," Prudence said gently, "we are surrounded by part of our family at the moment. We have no reason to keep secrets from them. In fact, we wouldn't be truly family members if we did."

"Well, yes, you have a point," Charity said. "All right, young ladies, spill your secrets, or you lose your membership in this family. Fair is fair."

Andrea laughed. "Sorry, Aunt Charity, but I'm fresh out of secrets."

"Me, too," Janice said, smiling.

All eyes turned toward Megan.

This is it, Megan thought. Everyone was just having fun, like playing Truth or Dare because they were at a birthday party, but there would never be a better opportunity to tell her *family* the real circumstances of her life. *Courage, Megan. You can do it.*

She lifted her chin. "I came to Prescott because I was running away from Charles, my ex-husband and a man who hopes to be governor, because he… physically and emotionally abused me."

Megan took a shuddering breath.

"That is my secret, and I want you to know the truth," she said, "because being a member of this family means more to me than I can ever begin to tell you."

"Bless you, dear," Aunt Prudence said. "My heart goes out to you, but you're safe now. All that you suffered through is behind you."

"Not yet," Megan said, her voice trembling. "The man in Sleeping Beauty yesterday wasn't making a pass at me. He was delivering threats from Charles."

"We'll shoot the bum," Aunt Charity said. "No, that's too quick and easy. We'll run him out of the state on a rail, the snake. Governor? Ha, my patootie. We'll cook his turkey. Once the press knows what he did to you, Megan, he'll be dead meat."

"Cook his goose," Aunt Pru said. "Not turkey, Charity. Goose. And that's poultry, not meat."

"Don't get picky, Pru," Charity said. "We'll kick his butt."

"That's what *I* said," Andrea said, smiling. "And I attributed that statement to you, Aunt Charity. Brandon and I knew about this yesterday, because Ben wanted Brandon to watch over Megan while she was in Sleeping Beauty. As it turned out, it was a good thing that Brandon was on red alert."

"So?" Aunt Charity said, looking at Megan again. "When are you calling a press conference?"

The women had been concentrating so intently on the conversation, they hadn't seen Ben approach. He placed both hands on Megan's shoulders as he stood behind her. She jumped slightly, unaware that he was near.

"Megan hasn't reached a decision about that yet, Aunt Charity," he said. "That's not the only choice available to her."

"Don't be silly, Benjamin," Aunt Charity said. "If Megan keeps silent, that polecat might end up being governor of Arizona."

"Charles Chastain might also choose to remarry," Aunt Prudence said quietly. "May the saints help that unknowing young woman, whoever she may be."

Megan stiffened. "I hadn't thought of that possibility."

"Cable Montana did," Ben said, tightening his hold on Megan's shoulders. "He dropped that bomb on me about a half an hour ago."

"Oh, dear heaven," Megan whispered.

"Don't upset yourself, dear," Aunt Prudence said, leaning over and patting Megan's hand. "I do believe, however, that you know, deep within yourself, what you must do.

"You think about it, and always remember that your family is here to support you. You're not alone, Megan, not anymore." She straightened and looked at Ben. "Isn't that right, Ben?"

Ben nodded. "That's right, Aunt Prudence. Megan is not alone."

"Neither are you, Benjamin," Aunt Prudence said, looking at him intently. "We've been your family for so many years, you may have forgotten that we're here for you, as well."

"Yep," Aunt Charity said. "We sure are. We're playing true confessions here, Ben. If you don't come clean with your secret, we'll boot you out of the clan."

"What secret?" Janice said. "Ben, do you have a secret? Am I missing something?"

"Yeah," Ben said, producing a small smile that didn't reach his eyes. "A biggie. The truth is...I have a fetish for toy trucks. If Joey doesn't watch out, I'm going to cop the one that Megan and I gave him today."

"Oh, pot," Aunt Charity said, frowning. "What a bunch of bull."

"Charity, please," Prudence said, "mind your language. You do upset my sensibilities when you speak like that. Tsk, tsk, shame on you."

"Well, for mercy's sake," Aunt Charity said. "You know yourself, Pru, that Ben has had something heavy preying on his mind for months. It's time—"

"That Megan and I were leaving," Ben interrupted. "We forgot to buy her a jacket when we went shopping, and it's getting chilly. Come on, Megan. Let's go."

"Oh, Ben," Charity said, shaking her head.

Megan got to her feet and a moment later Andrea leveled herself upward.

"I arrived in Prescott in the middle of a snowstorm at Christmastime with no jacket," Andrea said, smiling. "Since then, Brandon has bought me more than I'll ever be able to use. I'm ready to get off of this folding chair and put my feet up. Why don't you and Megan come back to the hotel, Ben, and I'll give Megan a coat?"

"Thank you, Andrea," Megan said. "That's lovely of you. I certainly don't want Ben spending any more money on my wardrobe."

"Cripes, Megan," Ben said. "It doesn't matter how much—"

"Ben, please," she said. "I'll be more comfortable borrowing a jacket from Andrea for now."

"Whatever," he muttered.

Goodbyes were said and Andrea, Megan and Ben started off in search of Brandon.

"Ben," Aunt Prudence said.

He stopped and half turned to look at her.

"Yes?" he said, raising his eyebrows.

"Charity and I love you, you know," Aunt Pru said. "You *and* Megan."

"She's got that straight, big boy," Aunt Charity said. "And don't you forget it."

Ben looked at the aunts for a long moment, nodded, then walked away.

During the restoration of Hamilton House, Brandon had had two apartments constructed on the fifth

floor, one for himself and one for Aunt Prudence and
Aunt Charity.

When Megan, Ben, Andrea and Brandon entered
the apartment in the hotel, Ben glanced around.

"I'm continually impressed with how great these
apartments turned out, Brandon," he said. "Are you
still planning on buying a house, though?"

"Yep." Brandon swept one arm in the air. "Sit.
There's no need to rush off. Unfortunately, Andrea
and I haven't found what we're looking for. I'm beginning to think it might be better to get some land,
hire an architect, and have a house built to our spec-
ifications—the way you did, Ben."

Ben and Megan settled onto the sofa. Andrea sat
on a straight-back chair and propped her feet on a
footstool, as Brandon sank onto a large easy chair
close to her.

"That's better," Andrea said. "Oh, my poor,
puffy tootsies." She paused. "You've been pleased
with your house since you had it built, haven't you,
Ben?"

Ben nodded. "Very pleased."

"With just cause," Megan said, smiling. "It's a
lovely home."

Home, Ben thought. Yes, the house had, indeed,
been transformed into a home since Megan had taken
up residency there.

It would, he supposed, be simply a house again
once Megan concluded her unfinished business with
Chastain and went on her way. To start over and
create a fulfilling life…for herself.

"Brandon Hamilton," Andrea said, laughing. "You have lipstick on your cheek. I didn't notice it when we were driving over here. What on earth have you been up to when I wasn't looking?"

Brandon chuckled as he scrubbed his hand over the telltale evidence on his cheek.

"As we were leaving the party, I told Jennifer that I'd made arrangements for a couple of guys from the staff here to show up at her place. They'll load the tables and chairs she borrowed from the hotel into a truck, and do whatever other cleaning she wants done in the yard from the birthday bash."

"No wonder you received a kiss," Megan said, smiling. "That was a lovely thing to do. You have good taste in men, Andrea."

"I think so, too," Andrea said, smiling warmly at her husband.

Brandon shrugged. "Jennifer and Joey are family. I was able to make things easier for her so... Hey, that's what a family is about, right? We're here for each other."

Ben got to his feet. With a frown on his face and his hands shoved into his pockets, he roamed around the large room. The other three watched him with questioning expressions. He finally stopped his trek, standing by the end of the sofa.

"Everyone except me seems to have a handle on this family thing," he said quietly, then looked at Megan. "You reached out to your new family today at the party, Megan, when you told them the truth about Chastain, about what you've been through."

"Yes," she said, staring at him intently. "Yes, I did, Ben."

"Their reaction wasn't what I expected," Ben went on. "I thought they'd fawn and fuss, gush all over you with pity and—but it wasn't like that. You got sympathy, yes, but more important, they let you know they were there for you as you moved forward with your life."

"Yes, they were wonderful," Megan said.

"I think…I think it's time," Ben said, "that I reached out to my family, too."

"Oh, Ben," Megan said softly. "Yes."

Ben looked up at the ceiling, took a deep breath, then let it out slowly before directing his attention to Andrea and Brandon.

"Andrea, Brandon," Ben said, "there's something you need to know." He shook his head. "No, let me rephrase that. There's something I need to share with you."

"Ben," Megan said, extending one hand toward him.

He hesitated, then joined her on the sofa, sitting close to her and placing her hand on his thigh, covering it with his own hand.

"What's going on, buddy?" Brandon said, frowning. "We've all been aware for months that you're struggling with something heavy. We've kept silent, but we've been here for you, you know."

"I thought I had to do this alone," Ben said. "But I was wrong." He looked at Megan. "I've been

shown by this lovely lady just how wrong I was."
He shifted his gaze back to Andrea and Brandon.

"I...that is, at some point in the future, I won't
be able to...what I mean is..." Ben stopped speaking
and shook his head. "Ah, hell, I'm going to be blind.
I'll no longer be able to see." His grip on Megan's
hand tightened.

"What?" Brandon said, leaning forward in his
chair. "What!"

"Dear heaven," Andrea whispered.

"Okay, okay," Brandon said, raising both hands.
"Let's take it from the top. All the details, Ben."

This was so difficult for him, Megan thought,
fighting against threatening tears. But he was doing
it, baring his soul, reaching out to his family as he
should have done months ago. Oh, how she loved
him.

"All right," Ben said, sounding suddenly weary.
"Here's the story."

With a voice gritty with emotion, Ben told Andrea
and Brandon what was happening to his brothers,
about the frustration of his doctor friend, who was
researching what remained a mystery, of the loss of
his own sight that would surely take place sometime
in the future.

"That's it," he said finally. "Now you know."

"I hate it," Brandon said, a rough edge to his
voice. "This isn't acceptable. No. No way. There has
to be something they can do to stop this from happening to you, Ben."

"I've been down the denial and anger road already, Brandon," Ben said. "It's a dead end."

"Ben," Andrea said, her voice trembling slightly. "I'm so terribly sorry. That doesn't begin to express how I feel, but there's no purpose to be served by my going on and on. I'm just...just so very sorry."

Ben nodded. "Thank you. I appreciate that. I'm going to ask you two to tell the aunts, Jennifer, Taylor and Janice, because I can't go through this tale of woe over and over. I realize that I'm placing a tremendous burden on you by that request, but..."

"You are not," Brandon said. "We'll take care of it."

"You said you have no symptoms yet?" Andrea said. "None?"

"No, nothing," Ben said. "I'm supposed to check in with my brothers to see how they are, but I keep putting it off because I really don't want to know. I'll do it, though. Soon."

Andrea sighed. "Well, let's be grateful that you're in the profession you are."

"I don't mean to be rude, Andrea," Ben said, his voice rising, "but you're crazy. I can't be a doctor when I'm blind. Think about it. I can't fix what I can't see."

"No, but there won't be anything wrong with your mind," Andrea said.

"Big deal," Ben said, none too quietly. "What good is that going to do me?"

"You can teach, Dr. Rizzoli," Andrea said, matching his volume. "You can share the vast knowledge you have, the years of experience, with the healers, the doctors of tomorrow.''

"Yes," Megan said. "Oh, my goodness, there it is. Yes, teach, and also dictate endless, informative articles for medical journals.''

"Yeah, right." Ben laughed, the sound bitter and sharp. "How do I get to this ever-famous classroom so I can teach? Oh, I know. My nursemaid will wash and shave me, put on my clothes, take me by the hand and lead me there like a little kid. No, thanks. I'll pass."

"Ben, don't," Megan said gently. "It wouldn't be like that. People without sight can learn to be independent and productive. Somewhere in your mind you know that's true. You do."

Ben dragged both hands down his face. "I've had enough of this for today. Borrow a coat, jacket, whatever, from Andrea, and let's be on our way."

"All right." Megan got to her feet, then turned her head to look at Ben again. "We'll go home. Together."

Chapter Eleven

Later that night, Megan came down the stairs to find Ben sitting on the sofa. He was leaning forward, his elbows on his knees, the steeple he'd made of his fingers resting lightly against his lips.

Ben had been so quiet, so withdrawn, ever since they left Hamilton House hours before. He'd replied to her questions absently, had hardly touched his dinner and now, even with the physical distance between them, she could sense—feel—the thick wall he'd erected around himself.

It was understandable, she supposed. It had been so difficult for Ben to share the stark facts of his future with Andrea and Brandon. Now it was all out in the open. Ben could no longer hide from his reality because the people who cared about him knew the truth.

How glorious it had all been when she and Ben had existed in their crystal ball world. They lived in the now, made love in the now, had laughed, talked and shared in the now.

Megan crossed the room slowly, hesitated, then sat on the end of the sofa, a cushion away from Ben. Several silent minutes passed as Ben continued to stare into the leaping flames of the fire in the hearth.

"Ben," Megan finally said quietly.

Ben snapped his head around, clearly surprised to find Megan sitting there.

"I'm sorry," he said. "I didn't hear you come downstairs. I was deep in thought, I guess."

"You have been ever since we left Andrea and Brandon," Megan said.

Ben leaned back and stretched his arms across the top of the sofa, shifting his gaze to the fire again.

"I know," he said. "I haven't been very good company tonight." He paused. "It's funny, strange really. I feel...lighter somehow, since I told Andrea and Brandon about what's happening to me. It's like I've spread out my situation and handed each of them a chunk of it, and given more pieces to the aunts, Jennifer, Janice and Taylor, because I imagine they all know by now.

"It's as though I'm saying, 'Hey, this is too heavy of a load, so help me out here, people. Everyone take some of it, get the weight of it off my back.' Weird, huh?" Ben turned his head to look at Megan.

"No, not at all. That's what caring and sharing is all about. You know you're not alone, struggling to deal with your problems in solitude." Megan frowned. "But what about me, Ben? I wasn't on your list of those who have a piece of your grim puzzle."

"That's because you've had the whole damn thing dumped on you. You're here with me, sharing every crummy detail of it, day in, day out. The next time you fall off a mountain, you really ought to pick a better hero to rescue you."

"Oh, okay," Megan said, smiling. "I'll try to remember that." Her smile faded. "Ben, were you thinking of what Andrea said about becoming a teacher?"

"Don't go there, Megan," he said, getting to his feet. "Not tonight." He moved around the coffee table to stand in front of the fire, his back to Megan, his hands shoved into his pockets. "I'm not ready to look that far ahead yet."

"All right," she said. "I understand." She paused again. "Ben, while I was upstairs, I made two telephone calls. One was to Andrea to ask if I could borrow her car. The other was to my attorney. I'm...I'm going to Phoenix tomorrow."

Ben yanked his hands free of his pockets and spun around to face her, his heart beating wildly.

"You're leaving?" he said. Ah, Megan, no! Not yet. Not yet!

"Just for the day. I should be back home before dark. I hope I am, because I've never driven mountain roads before. It will be nerve-racking enough in the daylight without attempting it in the dark."

She wasn't leaving for good, Ben thought. She was

coming back, coming *home*. He had to calm down. *Easy does it, Rizzoli.*

"Why are you going to Phoenix?" he said.

"My attorney will escort me to the house I shared with Charles. It will be a one-time event, so I can collect some clothes and personal belongings. It will be the last time I ever step foot in that house."

"Wait just a damn minute here." Ben moved forward and sat on the edge of the coffee table, his knees touching Megan's. "I don't want you running the risk of encountering Chastain. No way, Megan. You're not going into that house alone."

"I won't be alone. I just told you. My attorney will be with me."

"How old is he?" Ben said, frowning.

"What?"

"You heard me. How old is your suit-and-tie guy?"

Megan shrugged. "Well, I don't know. Sixty? Sixty-five?"

"Ah, hell. What's he going to do if Chastain gets rough?"

"We have the law on our side," Megan said, her voice rising. "I have every right to be there, to remove what belongs to me."

"Big deal," Ben said, matching her volume. "There's also a law that says it's illegal for a man to beat up his wife. Chastain doesn't follow the rules, Megan. Come on. Use your head. You're not going into that house without me."

Megan scooted past Ben's knees and got to her feet, turning immediately to look at him.

"You'd like to be there, wouldn't you?" she said, none too quietly. "You're just itching to pop Charles in the chops. You want to do that, because it will satisfy some…some macho whatever it is within you. Well, forget it, Rizzoli."

Megan took a shuddering breath, then rushed on.

"It's bad enough," she said, "that your entire medical practice could be in jeopardy because of me, because of Charles's threats because I'm with you. I won't have you ending up in jail on charges of assault. I'd never forgive myself if that happened."

Ben got to his feet. "And I'd never forgive myself if something happened to you while you were down there. No. You're not going without me."

He dragged a restless hand through his hair.

"You get back on the telephone and call your attorney," he said, narrowing his eyes. "Tell him we'll be coming together tomorrow. That's it. That's the bottom line. I'm with you, or you don't go. Have you got that, Megan?"

Dear heaven, Megan thought, a sudden warmth suffusing her, caressing her heart, her mind, her very soul. Ben Rizzoli loved her. He did!

The anger and concern in his eyes, so readable on his face, spoke of so much more than just caring. He was in love with her, just as she was in love with him. Oh, how glorious, how—

"Damn it, Megan, say something," Ben shouted.

"There's no need to yell," Megan yelled.

"The hell there isn't. I'll holler the roof down if that's what it takes to get through to you."

"Will you promise not to punch Charles if we cross paths with him?" Megan said, planting her hands on her hips.

"No!"

"I rest my case," she said, folding her arms across her breasts. "You're not going."

"Then neither are you, sweetheart," Ben shot back.

"Damn it, Ben." Megan's eyes widened. "Now look what you made me do. I said 'damn.' I never swear, never." She burst into laughter. "You're a terrible influence on me, Dr. Rizzoli. Oh, good grief what a mess. We're squabbling like children on the playground."

Megan continued to smile as she shook her head. "This really isn't funny, but laughing is better than crying, and I'm so tired of crying." Her smile disappeared. "So very tired of crying."

Ben enclosed the distance between them and encircled Megan with his arms.

Megan wrapped her arms around Ben's waist and leaned her head on his shoulder, savoring the aroma of him, the solid strength of his body, the warmth from his massive frame. She sighed and tightened her hold, as if to never let him go again.

"Ah, Megan, Megan," Ben said, then inhaled the spring-fresh scent of her silky curls. "What am I going to do with you?"

Just love me forever, Megan thought dreamily,

losing herself in the essence of Ben. For better, for worse. In sickness and in health. Until death do us part. Just love me.

"Well," she said, not moving an inch away from him, "you were the one who said that because you found me in the woods you got to keep me. So...keep me."

Yeah, right, Ben thought. At that moment Megan might believe that she actually wanted to stay with him. That made sad sense, because he was still the barrier, the safety net, between her and Chastain. But that situation was coming quickly to a head and would be over very soon.

Then? Megan would take a clear look at what Dr. Ben Rizzoli could offer her. Or to be more precise, what he *couldn't* offer her. No, she wouldn't want to stay with him then. No way.

But for now, *in* the now, she was his. And nothing, by damn, was going to happen to her. Whatever it took, whatever he had to do, he would keep Megan out of harm's way.

"Megan..." Ben started.

"Yes, all right." She raised her head to meet his troubled gaze. "I'll call my attorney back and tell him that you're coming with me tomorrow. He said he'd notify the housekeeper about our arrival, because I no longer have a key to the house."

"You know the housekeeper will tell Chastain that you're coming."

"Maybe not," she said. "She was always very kind. She didn't say anything derogatory about

Charles to me, but there was a softness, a gentleness, about her when we spoke. I believe she knew what Charles was doing to me.''

''But she still works for him, Megan, must feel a certain sense of loyalty to him. Or he pays her so well she doesn't want to lose the position. It doesn't matter. We'll be prepared for whatever happens.''

Ben paused. ''Thank you for giving in on this. I realize that you're trying to stand on your own two feet as you begin your new life, but there are times when that just isn't the way to do it.''

''That applies to your situation too, Ben.''

''Mmm.''

Megan smiled. ''You and your famous 'mmm.' You speak volumes with that little sound.''

''Mmm.'' Ben brushed his lips over hers. ''Mmm.'' He traced the outline of her lips with the tip of his tongue. ''Mmm. Mmm. Mmm.'' Then he captured her mouth in a searing kiss.

Desire exploded within them, hot, licking flames like those crackling in the fireplace. Ben raised his head, took a sharp breath, then slanted his mouth in the opposite direction to claim Megan's lips once again.

I love you, Megan, Ben's mind hammered. *You're going to leave me. I know you are, but, heaven help me, I love you. For now, in this now, you... are...mine.*

Ben deepened the kiss as he slid his hands over the feminine slope of Megan's bottom, pressing her close, his arousal heavy against her.

A whimper of need whispered from Megan's throat as she returned the urgent, nearly rough kiss in total abandon.

Oh, Ben, her mind hummed. *I love you with all my heart. I know you love me, Ben, I just know you do. I want to stay by your side forever. Don't send me away, Ben. Please, please, please.*

A beeping sound coming from one of the end tables caused Ben to stiffen and break the kiss, muttering an earthy expletive in the process.

"What...what is that noise?" Megan said, then took a much-needed breath.

"My pager." Ben eased her away from his heated, aching body. "I'm on call for the emergency room at the hospital tonight."

"Oh. Well...Oh."

Ben chuckled. "May I quote you on that, ma'am?" He went to the table, picked up the pager to see the number on the tiny screen, then nodded. "Yep. Damn. I have to call in."

As Ben strode toward the telephone on the kitchen wall, Megan sank onto the sofa, aware suddenly of her trembling legs. She placed one hand on her heart, willing it to return to a normal tempo.

A few minutes later, Ben returned and hunkered down in front of her, barely missing the coffee table.

"I have to go," he said. "There's a possible heart attack waiting in emergency. Call your attorney while I'm gone. I'll be back as soon as I can." He raised up enough to plant a kiss on her lips. "Hold that thought."

"Mmm," Megan said.

Ben laughed, then moments later hurried out the front door. Megan sat perfectly still, savoring the lingering taste of Ben and allowing her mind to conjure delicious scenarios of what would transpire between them when he returned.

Time lost meaning as she sat there, a soft smile on her lips, her body tingling with desire that would be satisfied so exquisitely by the wondrous lovemaking she would share with Ben.

A sharp knock at the front door caused Megan to snap out of her sensuous haze.

"Ben probably forgot his key," she said, getting to her feet. "Why did he take it off the chain, silly man?"

Good heavens, she thought. She had no idea that she'd been sitting there long enough for Ben to tend to business at the hospital and return home. She'd floated off into a rosy, passion-laden, lovely place.

She rushed to the door and flung it open, a smile on her lips.

"Ben, I'm so glad—"

She stopped speaking as a chill swept through her.

"Charles," she said, hardly above a whisper. "Oh, God, no."

She tried to close the door but Charles's arm shot out and he gripped the edge of the door with one hand, pushing it inward as he moved into the room. Megan backed up several steps, unaware that she had hunched her shoulders in an attempt to curl into herself in a protective gesture. Her heart beat so wildly, it was actually painful.

Charles Chastain slammed the door and narrowed his eyes. He was wearing his signature custom-tailored suit. His blond hair was razor cut, every strand in perfect place.

"You've been a naughty girl, Megan," he said, a steely edge to his voice. "And I'm very angry with you for the inconvenience you've caused me."

I'm sorry...sorry...sorry, Megan's mind screamed. *Please, Charles, no, don't hit me. No...no...no... please...please...*

"Nothing to say in your defense, my dear?" Charles said, advancing slowly toward her. "To add to your sins, you've taken a lover, a man so lower class that he doesn't even bother to get a haircut when needed. The thought of him touching you sickens me."

Charles stopped in front of Megan and shook his head.

"It's all so sad, so tragic," he said. "You're obviously mentally unbalanced, as evidenced by these recent escapades of yours. I'm going to see to it that you receive the finest care possible in a place where you can't endanger yourself further by running away like an undisciplined child."

"No," Megan whispered. "No."

"I waited until your doctor left, waited to see if he'd return. Waited and watched you, Megan, as you sat staring into the hearth.

"Were you thinking of me? The man who worships the very ground you walk on. The man who'd been your devoted and loving husband. The man who is devastated about your mental collapse, about having to put you away in an institution for a very, very long time.''

Charles lunged forward and gripped Megan tightly on her upper arms, giving her a rough shake.

''How dare you behave in this manner?'' he said, a pulse beating wildly in his temple. ''You're fortunate that the reporters didn't find out about this prank of yours, or I'd be even more angry than I am. But you must be punished, Megan. You understand that, don't you?'' He shook her again. ''Don't you?''

The chilling veil of fear that had encased Megan disappeared in a sudden swish. Taking its place was a red haze of fury.

With a surge of physical and emotional strength she didn't even know she possessed, she thrust her hands against Charles's chest and pushed him away.

He staggered backward, nearly falling, but regained his balance quickly, curling his hands into tight fists.

''What I understand,'' she said, her voice amazingly steady, ''is that you are an evil man, Charles Chastain. You will never hit me or hurt me again. Never. You no longer have control over me. I'm free. *Free.*

''Your threats mean nothing. *You* are nothing. You're finished, Charles. I'm going to tell the reporters the truth about you. Everything. You'll never be governor, because you'll be in jail, serving a sen-

tence for spousal abuse. *I* am going to put *you* away
for a very, very long time."

"No!" Charles roared.

He raced forward, his large hands closing around
Megan's slender throat, then tightening, tightening.

She beat at him with her fists as black dots began
to dance before her eyes and a loud buzzing noise
echoed in her ears.

The front door thundered against the wall and seconds later, Charles's grip on her neck loosened, then
was gone.

"You bastard," Ben said.

He spun Charles around and delivered a stunning
blow to the center of Charles's face. Charles flew
backward, landing on the floor with a resounding
thud and covering his nose with both hands. Blood
poured between his fingers.

Megan sank to her knees, gasping for breath.

Ben reached down, dragged Chastain to his feet
by the lapels of his jacket, then slammed him against
the wall.

"Don't hit me again," Charles whimpered, still
holding his nose. "You broke my nose. It hurts. I'm
in pain. Please don't hit me again."

Ben pulled back one fist to deliver another punch.

"Ben, no," Megan said, her voice scratchy.
"Don't do it. Don't lower yourself to his level. *I'm*
going to destroy him. With words, Ben, with the truth
of what he is. I have the strength now to do that. It's
over. Oh, Ben, it's over. *I really am free. I'm free.*"

Ben didn't move as he reached deep within himself for self-control to dim the want, the burning need, to smash his fist into Chastain's face over and over again. He drew a shuddering breath and shoved Chastain away, watching the cowering man sink to the floor again.

"Ben?" Megan whispered.

Ben turned and hurried to her, scooping her from the floor and holding her tightly. She buried her face in the crook of his neck.

"Are you all right?" Ben said, his voice raspy.

"Yes, yes. You're here. I thought you went to the hospital."

"I did. The man had indigestion, wasn't having a heart attack, so I came right back."

"I lost track of time, I guess. Thank you, Ben, thank you."

"There's nothing to thank me for. I just finished up what you obviously had already dealt with. Are you really going to do it? Are you going to blow the whistle on Chastain, call a press conference and expose him for what he is?"

Megan lifted her head and Ben's jaw tightened as he saw the red marks on Megan's throat from Charles's hands.

"Yes," Megan said. "I'm going to do it. I have the courage and strength now, I truly do."

Ben looked directly into her eyes. "Then you'll be free, just as you said."

"Yes."

"That's good. Yeah, that's…good." He set her carefully on her feet.

And when she'd finished with the details, taken care of all that needed to be done to close the final door on her nightmare past, she'd leave him to begin a new life.

"I'll...I'll call Cable Montana and have him come pick up Chastain."

Ben looked at Charles where he sat huddled on the floor, pressing a blood-soaked handkerchief to his still-bleeding nose.

"Well," Ben said. "I got one pop at him."

"Don't even think about hitting him again," Megan said. "He's not worth it, Ben."

"I *can't* hit him again." Ben chuckled and shook his head.

"Why not?"

"Man, oh, man, Brandon is going to laugh himself silly when he hears about this."

"What are you talking about?" Megan said, obviously confused.

"I took my best shot, and guess what?" Ben rolled his eyes heavenward and moaned. "I broke my hand!"

Chapter Twelve

"If I borrow a purple crayon from Joey," Brandon said, grinning, "can I sign your cast, Ben? Huh? Huh? Can I? Pretty please?"

"Give it a rest, Hamilton," Ben said, glaring at him. "Now!"

"Well, cripes, you're no fun," Brandon said, then took a bite of his juicy steak.

It was Wednesday evening and Ben, Andrea, Brandon, and the aunts were enjoying a delicious dinner in the dining room at Hamilton House.

Jennifer was on duty as the hostess, but stopped often at the group's table to get caught up on all the details regarding Megan and the newsbreaking story of the downfall of Charles Chastain.

"Megan still doesn't know when she'll be able to come back to Prescott?" Andrea asked Ben.

"No." Ben attempted again to cut his steak despite the cumbersome cast on his right hand. "Damn." He dropped his knife and fork onto the plate.

"Shall I cut your meat for you, dear?" Aunt Prudence said.

"No." Ben sighed. "Yes. Thank you, Aunt Prudence. I'm a starving man here. I'll sure be more sympathetic when I slap casts on people in the future."

"One often has to walk in another's shoes," Aunt Pru said, "to truly understand their journey." She finished cutting Ben's steak and slid the plate back in front of him. "There you are, dear."

"Thank you." Ben paused. "I want to thank you, too, you and Aunt Charity, and Jennifer, for your...well, quiet reaction to what Brandon and Andrea told you about my eyesight. The hugs said enough, and I appreciate your not going on and on about it."

"We'll deal with it, big boy," Aunt Charity said, "when it happens."

Ben nodded.

"So!" Andrea said. "Back to Megan. We watched her press conference on television. She was dynamite."

"That she was," Ben said quietly. "Very strong. Very classy. She insisted on going to Phoenix alone, and standing on her own two feet. I put her on the puddle-jumper plane out at the airport on Sunday and off she flew."

"But she'll be back," Aunt Prudence said.

"Maybe," Ben said, directing his attention to his dinner.

"Maybe?" Andrea said, leaning slightly toward Ben.

"She said she'd be back Monday night after the press conference." Ben said, looking at Andrea. "This is Wednesday. Do you see her at this table? She told me on the phone last night that there's a bundle of stuff she has to tend to. Endless statements to the cops, and on and on."

"Well," Andrea said, "that's reasonable."

"She's also had endless calls from talk show hosts," Ben went on, "wanting her to be interviewed about spousal abuse."

"Did she agree to do the shows?" Andrea said.

"She didn't agree," Ben said. "But she didn't refuse, either. She told them she had too much to deal with at the moment, and she'd think about it."

"And you said?" Brandon prompted.

"Nothing," Ben said, lifting one shoulder in a shrug. "I didn't say anything really, except that she should do whatever felt right to her."

"Well, mercy sake, hotshot," Aunt Charity said. "That's not going to get Megan back under your roof and into your bed where she belongs."

"Charity, please," Aunt Prudence said. "You're being a trifle personal, dear."

"I am not," Aunt Charity said. "Anyone with half an ounce of sense knows that Ben and Megan are in love with each other, should be together. The way

Ben responded to what Megan said about all those television offers, it sounded as though he didn't give a rip if she came back to Prescott or not."

"Megan has the right to make her own decisions, Aunt Charity," Ben said.

"Megan has the right to have all the data she needs to make those decisions," Aunt Charity said, scowling at him. "Does she know you're in love with her?"

"*You* said that," Ben said, matching her expression. "*I* didn't."

"Oh, give me a break, big boy," Aunt Charity said. "Who are you trying to bluff? Yourself? You're in love with Megan Chastain, and you know it. Where you blew it is that you didn't tell *her* that."

"What's the point?" Ben said, his voice rising. "I have nothing to offer her. Nothing. A whole new life is opening up for Megan. She can do a helluva lot better than spending the remainder of her days with a blind man." Ben shook his head and pushed his plate away. "Hell."

An uncomfortable silence fell over the group and several minutes ticked by with no one looking at anyone else.

"I think," Brandon said finally, "that you're not listening to your own words, Ben."

"Meaning?"

"You said Megan has the right to make her own decisions," Brandon said quietly. "Aunt Charity has a valid point. Megan doesn't have all the data she needs to do that decision-making."

"Enough," Ben said wearily. "I feel like a bug under a microscope. Let's mind someone else's business for a while. Andrea, say something pregnant."

Andrea smiled. "I have to go to the bathroom."

"Thank you," Ben said, chuckling in spite of himself. "You may be excused."

"Go along with Andrea, Charity," Prudence said.

"Why?" Charity said. "I don't have to use the powder room."

"I know, dear, but Andrea needs to give you a stern lecture about not nagging our Ben. Now, shoo."

"Such silly people," Aunt Charity said, getting to her feet.

"I do believe I'll join you," Aunt Pru said.

Ben watched the three women walk away, then looked at Brandon.

"Well, that was as subtle as being hit by a rock," Ben said. "What's next on the grand agenda since the ladies cleared the deck? You whip a man-to-man routine on me about Megan?"

"Don't look at me," Brandon said, raising both hands. "I'm the last guy in the world who would claim to know how women's minds work. I don't have a clue as to what I'm supposed to do now that I have you alone."

"Good," Ben said gruffly. "Then just shut up and eat your dinner."

"Fine with me." Brandon paused. "Except..."

"Ah, hell, here it comes."

"Look, buddy," Brandon said, "all I know is this.

You were the one who sent me after Andrea when she left me and went back to Phoenix. If I hadn't gone after her like you urged me to do—hell, I don't even want to think about what might have happened. Or, to be more precise, what might *not* have happened."

"This is entirely different, Brandon."

"Why?"

"You had everything to offer Andrea. A future, that baby she's carrying right now. What's it going to take to get through to you people? My future is empty. Dark, cold and empty. If Megan's smart, she won't ever return to Prescott. She'll just cut ties with me now while she has the chance."

"Is that what you want?" Brandon said, staring at Ben intently.

Ben leaned back in his chair and looked up at the ceiling for a long moment. He took a deep, shuddering breath, let it out very slowly, then met Brandon's gaze again.

"No," Ben said, his voice raspy with emotion. "No, that's not what I want. Not even close. I want to marry Megan, have babies with her, be the best damn doctor I can be until I'm too old to function. Then? I want to grow old with the woman I love, bouncing grandchildren on my knee.

"But, Brandon, none of that is going to happen. None of it. I'm not going to be a husband, father, grandfather or doctor. All I'm going to be is blind. End of story. For the sake of our lifelong friendship, hear me talking. *The subject is closed.*"

Brandon nodded slowly. "I hear you, Ben."

"Good. Fine."

"I'm sorry," Brandon said, shaking his head. "I'm just so damn sorry."

"Yeah," Ben said, his voice hushed. "So am I. I was close, but no cigar, huh? Ah, well, that's life."

"It stinks," Brandon said.

"In spades."

The women returned to the table and the meal was completed with idle chitchat and gossip. Hugs and handshakes were exchanged in the lobby of the hotel, then Ben drove home.

Alone.

Megan signed her name to yet another document, then set the pen down firmly on the stack of papers.

"That's it," she said. "The last of it. I'm finished. And on a Friday. T.G.I.F. I'm done."

"Indeed you are," her attorney said. "Except for testifying at Charles's trial when it's scheduled. That's no doubt months away, though. What are your plans now, Megan?"

She got to her feet, a lovely smile lighting up her face.

"I'm getting into my packed-to-the-maximum car," she said, "and driving up the mountain to Prescott. I'm going home." She laughed with pure joy. "To Ben."

Ben finished making notes in a patient's folder, then tossed it onto the stack waiting to be filed. The office was quiet after a particularly hectic day. The work week was over, and Sharon and Cynthia had told him to have a nice weekend before the two women had left the building.

A nice weekend? Ben thought. Fat chance.

He shook his head in self-disgust and dragged both hands down his face.

If he didn't get a grip, no one would want to be around him.

Enough was enough. He was overdue to shape up and start working on accepting things as they stood.

First on the agenda would be to call his brothers, which he would do before the weekend was over. The update on the condition of their sight might give him a clearer picture of the time frame he was facing before his own eyesight began to diminish.

Then he had to start dealing with his reality.

A reality that included the fact that Megan was not going to return to Prescott, to him.

He knew that was true because for the first time since he'd put Megan on the plane for Phoenix, she hadn't called him to say good-night. The previous evening had been a seemingly endless series of empty hours waiting for the telephone to ring. But it never did.

Ben sighed and leaned back in his leather chair.

Megan was doing the right thing. He knew that. She was physically separated from him in Phoenix, and now she was starting the emotional distancing, as well.

She was realizing, he was certain, that her entire

life lay before her like a lush buffet just waiting for her to pick and choose what she wanted to do with her future.

A future that would not include being saddled with a blind lover who had nothing to offer her.

Yes, Megan was doing the right thing by backing off from him. Damn it, he knew that. But, oh, man, it hurt. He missed her, ached for her, for the sound of her laughter, the sparkle in her big, blue eyes, her aroma of sunshine, fresh air and flowers. The feel of her soft body nestled next to him through the hours of the night.

Would the day come when the memories of what he'd shared with Megan would bring him a sense of warmth, of knowing he had experienced a love that was rich, and real, and honest? He hoped so, because the remembrance of the wondrous days and love-making nights with Megan would be all that he would have.

Accept it, Rizzoli. He had to start acting like a man about his fate, instead of a child.

He had to begin to think about how he would fill his days when he could no longer see, what he would do to justify his existence.

Teach, Andrea had said. Share with the physicians of tomorrow what he had learned, the knowledge he had. Make his years as a doctor continue to count for something, even though he could no longer practice medicine himself.

Teach. Maybe, just maybe, there was something

solid there to hang on to. Something that might possibly give meaning and purpose to his life. Maybe.

What he did know for certain was that Megan had gathered her inner courage and squared off against her past with class and dignity. And he, by damn, would do the same thing regarding his future. Somehow.

Ben left the office and drove toward his house. As the A-frame came into view, his eyes widened and his heart seemed to actually skip a beat.

Smoke was curling from the chimney and a late-model blue BMW was in the driveway. Ben parked next to the expensive vehicle and saw that the passenger and back seats were filled with boxes and suitcases.

Megan? his mind thundered. *Megan?*

He ran to the front door, fumbled a second getting the key in the lock, then burst into the living room, slamming the door behind him.

"Megan?" he called.

She appeared from the kitchen area, a bright smile on her face.

"Ben!" she said.

They moved at the same time, rushing to close the distance between them, meeting in the center of the room. Megan flung herself into Ben's arms, causing him to stagger slightly. Her hands encircled his neck; his arms wrapped around her waist to pull her close.

Their lips joined in a kiss that was an explosion of senses.

I'm home, Megan's heart and mind sang.

Megan was home, Ben thought hazily.

The kiss went on, and on, and on.

Ben finally raised his head to take a rough breath.

"You're here," he said, his voice gritty. "I thought...I mean, when you didn't call last night I—"

"I wanted to surprise you," Megan said, her own voice slightly husky with desire. "I knew I would finish everything I needed to do in Phoenix today, and I was afraid to speak with you in fear that I wouldn't be able to keep from telling you that I'd be driving up this afternoon." She smiled. "Are you glad to see me?"

"Nope," Ben said, matching her smile. "I greet anyone who happens to be hanging around my house the way I just said hello to you."

"Ah," she said, laughing. "No wonder Nutmeg the cat keeps coming to see you. Oh, Ben, I've missed you. It seems like I've been gone for an eternity. So much has taken place since I got on that little plane and flew down to the valley." She paused. "How's your hand?"

Ben released his hold on her reluctantly, then held up his right hand.

"It's a nuisance. Mike Hunt is going to switch this cast to one of those lightweight numbers in a week or so. That will help the situation. Hey, something sure smells good in here...besides you."

"That's part of my surprise. I stopped at the grocery store on the way through town. We're having lamb chops, baby peas, mashed potatoes, salad, and cherry cheesecake for dessert. I used the house key in the phony rock in the back yard that you showed me and—ta-da—here I am.''

For how long? Ben's mind yelled. Was her car still loaded because she hadn't had time to unpack, or was she just passing through on the way to wherever she planned to start her new life?

Damn it, Rizzoli, get a grip. He'd already determined that Megan wouldn't—*shouldn't* stay with him. She needed to move on. It was the best thing, the only thing, for her to do that made any sense.

But, oh, man, he was glad to see her. For now, Megan was home.

''Are you hungry?'' Megan said. ''Dinner is just about ready. I was crossing my fingers that you wouldn't work late.''

''I'm a starving man.''

''Wonderful. Go wash up and I'll start putting this banquet on the table.''

Ben dropped a quick kiss on her lips, then strode from the room. Megan returned to the kitchen and began to transfer the hot food to serving dishes.

She was so nervous, she thought. Even though she'd been busy preparing dinner, she hadn't been able to keep her apprehension at bay.

She was no longer Megan with amnesia, nor Megan Chastain, who lived in fear that Charles would find her. She was a woman whose entire future stretched before her.

She was free.

Everything was different, changed. She didn't

need Ben to protect her from her past, from the evil man who had terrified her. Ben had provided her with a safe haven, a port in the storm, but the storm was over.

She mustn't assume that she was still welcome to stay with Ben, to remain by his side. Her worldly goods were still in her car because she wasn't certain that Ben wanted her there.

How would she broach the subject? What should she say? Good heavens, she had so many butterflies swishing in her stomach, she'd never be able to eat a bite of this meal she'd prepared.

Ben came into the kitchen. "Put me to work."

"No, no, you sit down," Megan said. "Everything is ready."

Ben settled onto one of the chairs at the table and watched Megan bustle back and forth with the serving dishes. He drank in the sight of her, allowing himself the luxury of letting the warmth within him fully consume him.

Enjoy it while you can, he told himself. Megan couldn't stay here, even if she wanted to, because while her life was completely changed, his wasn't.

Megan sat opposite Ben.

"There," she said. "I hope you enjoy it."

"And I hope you don't mind cutting my meat. Until I get the softer cast on this hand, I'm at the mercy of someone with a willing fork and knife."

"My pleasure, sir."

The task completed, Ben ate in silence for several minutes.

"Delicious, and I thank you," he said finally. "Hey, you haven't taken a bite yet."

"Oh." Megan shoveled in a forkful of potatoes.

"So," Ben said. "Bring me up to date on your doings. I know you've put the television interview offers on hold. I know you have a restraining order against Charles."

Megan nodded. "I'm still stalling in regard to the interviews. I just haven't had time to really think it through yet.

"As for the restraining order, Charles's attorney has assured me that Charles has no intention of violating that order. He's in enough trouble, because I intend to testify against him at his trial when it's scheduled. He's out on bail, but he's hiding from the press somewhere. He's finished, Ben. He'll never be governor."

"Thanks to you. I told you on the phone, but I'll say it again," Ben said. "What you did took a great deal of courage, and I'm awed by everything you've done."

"It was the thought of Charles remarrying, of abusing another woman, that gave me the strength to see it through to its proper end," Megan said quietly. "I just have to wait to testify at the trial. In my mind, though, I'm free."

Ben nodded. "Yes. Yes, you are."

"I signed documents today regarding a new settlement in connection with the divorce."

"Oh?"

"I told my attorney that I didn't want anything

except my personal belongings and the small amount of money I'd brought to the marriage so I would have a nest egg to begin my new life. He convinced me I was making an enormous mistake.''

''Oh?'' Ben repeated.

''He said that the original settlement had been grossly unfair, that this was a community property state and, heaven knew, I'd earned a right to my half of Charles's assets. He went on and on about how I should be able to do whatever I wished now and deserved more than just a little nest egg.''

Ben nodded. ''He's right. I guess I underestimated your old suit-and-tie guy.''

''Well, I finally agreed and…and it would seem that I'm going to be a very wealthy woman, Ben. Stocks will be liquidated, the house and other properties sold, and so forth. I opened a special account where the money can be deposited. I came away with a huge sum already from the checking and savings accounts.''

''Ah, there we go,'' Ben said, waggling his eyebrows at her. ''I am now officially after your money.''

''Okay,'' Megan said with a shrug, then laughed. ''Oh, my, so much has happened so quickly that my head is spinning. I think I need some time for it all to sink in.''

''Mmm,'' Ben said. ''That makes sense. It's wise, too. You shouldn't make any hasty decisions.''

''Or I'll repent in leisure?''

''However that saying goes,'' he said, looking directly at her. "You need to consider all your options, Megan. You can do—be—anything you wish."

Megan averted her gaze from Ben's and fiddled with her spoon.

"Would...would you care to make any suggestions," she said, "as to what I might do?"

"It wouldn't be right for me to do that, Megan. It's your life, your future."

Megan sighed and looked at him again. "Ben, I don't have the experience, or sophistication, to be coy about this. All I can be is me, speak from my heart, be honest." She drew a shuddering breath. "I...I love you, Ben Rizzoli. I want to stay here, with you. That's what I wish, what I want, with all my heart. I truly love you, Ben."

Yes! Ben thought.

No! his mind hammered in the next instant.

"I...um...don't know quite what to say here, Megan. I'm very flattered, believe me, but—"

"But you don't love me," Megan said, attempting and failing to produce a smile. Quick tears filled her eyes and she got to her feet. "That's clear enough. Silly me, I thought you did love me.

"Would you like some cherry cheesecake? I'll clean the kitchen, then head into town and see if there's a room available at Hamilton House. A suite, maybe. Heaven knows, I can afford it. Yes, that's what I'll do. I'll pamper myself with room service and—"

"Damn it, Megan," Ben said, lunging to his feet and nearly toppling his chair over. "Stop it." He moved around the table to grip her shoulders, the cast a heavy weight where his hands landed. "Don't do this."

"Don't do what, Ben?" she said, tears shimmering in her eyes. "I'm accepting the fact that you don't return my feelings in kind. I'm attempting to be very adult about this. There's nothing for you to be so angry about. It's no one's fault that you don't love me as I love you."

"Don't love you?" he hollered. "What do you think this has all meant to me? Everything we've shared, been through together? What kind of man do you believe I am? Not love you? Ah, hell, Megan, I love you more than I could ever begin to put into words. I—damn it, what am I doing? Saying?"

Ben stepped back and dragged his uninjured hand through his hair.

"You…you love me?" Megan whispered, dashing two tears from her cheeks. "You're in love with me?"

"Yes. No. Forget it," Ben said, shaking his head. "It doesn't matter."

"Doesn't matter?" Megan gripped Ben's biceps and looked at him intently. "How can you say that? We're in love with each other, Ben. How can that possibly not matter?"

"Megan, wake up," he said, a pulse beating rapidly in his temple. "Everything has changed for you. You…are…free. The demons of your past are gone. You have your whole life ahead of you. *Nothing* has changed for me. I still have no future, nothing to offer you. *I'm going to be blind.*''

"I know that, Ben," she said softly.

"Do you? Really?" he shot back. "Or are you going around in a rosy glow? Damn it, Megan, what I'm facing is why my feelings for you don't matter. I'm not free of my demons and I never will be. Your future is not with me. It's not.''

"Are…are you sending me away?''

"I can't ask you to stay," he said, his voice rough with emotion.

"And if I choose to stay?''

"Don't be a fool, Megan. Get in your fancy car and go, as fast and as far as you can.''

"Is that what you want, Ben?" she said, tears echoing in her voice.

"Megan, please, you're ripping me up," he said, shaking his head. "What I want? I want it all, lady. I want to marry you, watch you grow big with my baby nestled inside you, spend the rest of my life with you.

"But, Megan? I want to *see* you every morning when I wake up. *See* our child's first smile, first steps. *See* you when we're old and gray, and playing with our grandchildren. *I want to see.*''

"Oh, Ben," Megan said, a sob catching in her throat.

"Megan, make a life for yourself somewhere else, with someone else. Get everything you deserve to have. Do it, Megan.''

A shiver coursed through her, then she lifted her chin.

"Perhaps you're right," she said. "I'm reacting from emotion, instead of logic."

"No joke," Ben said, a bitter edge to his voice.

"However," she said, pointing one finger in the air, "we've established the fact that I shouldn't do anything hasty. I've had a great deal heaped on my plate at once, and I need to consider all my options. Therefore…" She tapped her finger against her chin.

"Therefore?" Ben said, narrowing his eyes.

"No past, no future…just now. You were the one who initially said we should exist in the now. Correct? Right." Megan shrugged and smiled. "So, we'll keep doing that until I figure out where to go and what to do with my newfound freedom and wealth."

"What are you up to, Megan?" Ben said, studying her intently.

"Nothing," she said breezily. "We've done it before, we can do it again, Ben. Just live in the now, the moment at hand."

"I—"

"Unless, of course," she went on, "you'd prefer that I take up residency in Hamilton House while I ponder my future."

"No!"

"Well, that settles that, doesn't it?" she said, smiling brightly.

"Megan—"

"So, Dr. Rizzoli, here we are again in our lovely

crystal ball world, and I have one final question to ask you."

"What is it?"

"Would you like some cherry cheesecake or not?"

Chapter Thirteen

Megan paced around Andrea and Brandon's living room, alternating between wringing her hands and flinging her arms out in expressive gestures as she related her story to an attentive Andrea.

"I just bluffed my way through at that point," Megan said, spinning around and retracing her steps. "I didn't give Ben a chance to say much of anything about our living for the moment, because I just kept blithering on and on."

"Good for you," Andrea said, nodding decisively. "Then what?"

"Then?" Megan flung her arms out again. "Ben sat down and ate a piece of cherry cheesecake."

Andrea laughed. "Oh, my."

"He looked rather dazed," Megan rushed on.

"Sort of like he'd been run over by a bulldozer that he hadn't seen coming."

"Megan, why don't you sit down?" Andrea said. "I think you've walked three miles since you arrived here."

"Oh." Megan slouched onto the sofa. "Ben loves me, Andrea, just as I love him, but he was fully prepared to send me away, to end our relationship, because he will be losing his sight."

"Are you certain you're prepared to spend the rest of your life with a man who can't see?" Andrea said gently.

"Of course I am. I love him. He'd still be my Ben, no matter what. There's no disclaimer on my love that says it will end at the moment Ben loses his sight. How can you ask such a question?"

"Just checking." Andrea paused. "How did things go between you two the remainder of the weekend?"

"Just beautifully," Megan said rather dreamily. She blinked and blushed a pretty pink. "What I mean is, Ben was fine. He seemed relaxed, happy, chatted about this and that. We went for a long walk in the woods, watched old movies, cooked together.

"There were no more heavy discussions. Things were like they were before I left for Phoenix. It was strange, very strange."

"Not really," Andrea said. "Ben loves you, Megan, and is apparently eager to postpone your leaving for as long as possible."

"But I don't want to leave at all," Megan said

sadly. "I want to stay with Ben forever. Our now is supposedly going to end when I decide what I wish to do with my newfound freedom."

Andrea laughed. "Do you suppose Ben would notice if you didn't make a decision during the next fifty years?"

"This situation," Megan said, sitting bolt upright, "is *not* funny."

"I know, I know," Andrea said, once again serious. "You've bought yourself some time, but the problem hasn't been solved.

"Ben has to realize that he can have a very fulfilling and productive life whether he has his sight or not. He also has to believe that he has every right to the happiness you two would have together."

"Oh, is that all?" Megan said dryly.

"Megan, my friend," Andrea said, "I don't have a magic wand to fix this mess. We can only hope that time is the answer. You're there with Ben, sharing, caring, loving. That's all you can do. Ben has to find his own inner peace, and come to grips with his reality."

"What if…I'm not one of the pieces?" Megan said, struggling against sudden threatening tears. "What if he sends me away, after all?"

"Don't get gloomy, Megan. Men can be very dense and stubborn, but when the chips are down in regard to their hearts, they seem to do the right thing. Brandon did. He came after me, drove down to Phoenix to ask me to marry him. Ben was the one who pushed Brandon to do that. Ben knew it was what needed to be done.''

"Mmm," Megan said.

"You sound like Ben when you do that," Andrea said, smiling. "Let's give Ben some credit here. He has a lot to deal with right now, but we have to believe he'll figure it all out and do what needs to be done. Time is on your side. Use it well."

Megan nodded. "Thank you, Andrea, for listening to me."

"That's what friends—family—do. We all love you and Ben. We'll be hoping—praying—that you two get a happy ending, just as Brandon and I did."

"Me, too," Megan said, getting to her feet. "I must go. I'm supposedly at the library researching career opportunities. I'd better have something to report at dinner tonight."

"Do you have any idea what you really want to do?"

"Yes, actually I do," Megan said, nodding. "There's a wonderful shelter here in Prescott for battered women. I thought I'd open a shop that sells used clothes, toys, furniture—everything—with the profits going to the shelter. I'll fix up the store so it's a fun place to browse. I'd advertise and urge people to clean house and donate their goodies."

"What a marvelous idea."

"I'm going to start looking for just the right storefront to set up business. But, oh, heavens, Ben mustn't know that I've reached a decision about what I intend to do."

"Good grief, no, not yet. My lips are sealed, except for telling Brandon. Ben needs this time to find the answers to his questions."

"Time," Megan said. "It's all I have going for me."

"No, Megan, you also have love on your side and that is very powerful stuff. Don't forget that."

"Yes. Yes, you're right. I just hope it's enough."

Ben choked on a sip of soda and coughed, finally having to thump himself on the chest.

"Chickens?" he said incredulously, when he could speak. "You're thinking about raising chickens?"

"Chickens are nice," Megan said. "Goodness, this Chinese food you brought with you is delicious. Too bad I have no idea what I'm eating. Oh, well, it tastes good."

"Back to the chickens," Ben said, pointing his fork at her.

"I brought home a whole stack of books from the library on the care and feeding of chickens," Megan said. "There's a vast market for homegrown eggs, you know."

Ben chuckled and shook his head. "Homegrown eggs? I've never heard it put quite like that before. So, okay, where would you raise these feathery fortune makers?"

"I'd buy some land here in Prescott that is zoned for chickens, have cute little houses built for them and, bingo, I'm off and running in the egg business."

"Mmm," Ben said.

"Andrea could work up some super advertising for me," Megan blithered on. "If she and Brandon became one of my customers, they could say on the menus that Hamilton House serves fresh, homegrown eggs."

"That ought to have people standing in line to eat breakfast at the hotel."

"Sure." Megan frowned. "There's just one teeny tiny problem."

"Oh?" Ben said, raising his eyebrows.

"I'm allergic to feathers."

"Forget the chickens, Megan."

"Right."

Late the next afternoon, Ben walked slowly along the campus of Yavapai Community College, located near the edge of town.

He was early for his appointment with the representative from the University of Arizona, he knew, but he was enjoying the stroll in the crisp fall air, and the chance to unwind from a busy day at the office.

Chickens, he thought suddenly, causing him to chuckle. Oh, man, Megan was really something. He had to give her credit, though, for diving right in and exploring her career options.

But, chickens? No, she'd come up with another, more sensible plan, one where she should direct her intelligence and drive.

Megan loved him. She honest-to-goodness loved

him, and he loved her more than he could ever describe in words.

He frowned as he continued to walk.

Their love for each other, however, didn't change what had to be the final outcome of their relationship. He would eventually have to end it, send her away, tell her to get on with her life and forget him.

Megan was convinced that she could live with the fact that he would be blind at some point in the future. But he didn't quite buy her quick agreement that she wasn't thinking past her emotions. He had a feeling she was humoring him, waiting for him to change his stand on the issue.

He didn't doubt that she believed his losing his sight would make no difference to them as long as they were together.

Well, it made a difference to *him.*

Megan deserved better than what he would become. She should have a complete man for a husband, one who could give her a child, then stand by her side to watch—*see*—their baby grow into a happy, healthy adult.

Bottom line? He loved Megan far too much to allow her to stay with him. Once she'd settled on a career, what he and Megan had together would be over.

"So be it," he said under his breath.

Ben entered the proper building. Ten minutes later, he was sitting in a small office opposite a man behind a desk.

Professor Wilson was in his mid-fifties, portly, nearly bald, and had a laid-back, friendly demeanor.

Ben was instantly comfortable, and twenty minutes went by quickly as Ben spoke, the professor listening attentively.

"There you have it," Ben said finally. "I can't give you a timetable on this proposal because...my friend has no idea when this menace will strike him, but...well, the evidence is all there that he'll definitely be blind at some point in the future."

Professor Wilson nodded. "That's rough. However, I admire the fact that...your friend is already exploring avenues that might be open to him when he can no longer see and function as a physician."

Ben propped one ankle on his opposite knee. "So, what do you think?"

"As far as I'm concerned," the professor said, "it's a done deal. I'll hire him in a heartbeat when he's ready. We're getting this satellite campus of the U of A going here at Yavapai. To be able to offer a lecture series in the area of medicine would be fantastic for us."

"Oh."

"You seemed surprised, Dr. Rizzoli."

"Ben. It's Ben. He'll...my friend...will be blind."

"So? His years of hands-on experience will be invaluable to medical students. We'd need a course outline. I'd take that to the powers that be, and we'd iron out the wrinkles with your friend so that the class would qualify for credit for the students, then we'd be up and running."

"Oh." Ben shook his head. "I sound like a parrot. It's just that I didn't think this idea would be so well received. I mean—hell, I don't know."

"Ben, did you notice that I didn't stand up to shake your hand when you came into this office?"

Ben lifted one shoulder in a shrug. "No, I really didn't think about it one way or another."

"Well, I couldn't rise to greet you because I'm paralyzed from the waist down. I was in an automobile accident ten years ago that killed my wife and daughter, and left me unable to walk."

"I'm sorry," Ben said, dropping his foot to the floor. "I really am."

"So am I," Professor Wilson said. "For the first year after the accident I wanted to die. I'd lost everything of meaning to me—my wife, child, my career as a professor of anthropology that took me out into the field with my students.

"Oh, I went through the motions, attended my physical therapy classes, as well as those that were designed to show me how to function on my own, but my heart wasn't in it. I was so angry and bitter at the injustice of what had happened to me."

Ben leaned slightly forward. "But you're here in a very productive and worthwhile career position. What changed your attitude, your outlook?"

Professor Wilson chuckled. "A woman. My physical therapist. One day she blew a fuse. She got in my face and told me she'd had enough of me. I either shaped up and counted my blessings, or she was quitting. She quite literally saved my life, right then and there.''

"I'll be damned," Ben said.

"A year later, she and I were married."

"What?"

"Yep. I'm a happy man, Ben. Oh, I still remember the wonderful years I had with my first wife, still mourn for my daughter and all the living she never had a chance to do, but my existence today is rich, full, and I'm sharing it with a woman I love very deeply." Professor Wilson glanced at his watch. "I have another appointment, I'm afraid."

Ben got to his feet and reached across the desk to shake the older man's hand.

"Thank you," Ben said. "Thank you very, very much, Professor."

"My pleasure. And, Ben? When you lose your sight, my office door will be open, waiting for you to walk through it. There's a place for you here. Remember that."

"You knew all along I was talking about myself, didn't you?"

"Yes," the professor said. "Because I heard the echo of anger, the self-pity, the frustration in your voice, saw it all in your eyes, as you were relating the story of your *friend.*

"You remind me of myself, Ben, many years ago. Let those destructive emotions go, son. You have a long life ahead of you that will be different from what you've known, but no less meaningful."

"I—"

"Think about it."

Ben nodded, then turned and walked from the room.

That evening Ben reread a paragraph in a medical journal for the third time and realized he still had no idea what it said.

Megan was nestled close to him on the sofa, leafing through a fashion magazine showing a vast array of winter clothes.

"The fire is getting low," Ben said. "Needs a couple more logs."

"Mmm," Megan said, her attention directed toward the glossy pictures. "Plum. Eggplant. Salsa. They're actually using those names to describe the colors of some of these outfits."

"Megan," Ben said, turning his head to look at her. "What if I was paralyzed, incapable of getting up, going outside and toting in logs for the fire?"

Megan frowned as she met his gaze. "Where did that come from out of the blue?"

"Just answer the question."

"Well," she said with a shrug, "I'm perfectly capable of carrying in firewood. I'd just trot myself out there and get what we needed."

"Okay, but try this one on for size. I couldn't go up the stairs to the bedroom."

"We'd get a house that's all on one floor, or install a lift that would zoom you up the stairs."

"I couldn't drive."

"Sure you could," she said. "They convert vehicles to have the brakes and gas pedals workable from the steering wheel. If you couldn't walk, we'd deal with it the best way possible.'' She paused. ''Am I missing something? Why are we having this conversation?''

Ben got to his feet and began to roam restlessly around the room.

''Take it deeper, Megan,'' he said. ''Make it real in your mind. I can't walk, will never be able to walk. You'd be out of here, right? Long gone.''

Megan smacked the magazine onto the coffee table.

''That's the most insulting thing I've ever heard,'' she said, nearly shouting. ''I love you, Ben. Don't you even have a clue as to what that means?

''In sickness and in health, until death do us part. Whether or not you were capable of walking— *whether or not you could see*—I would not...I repeat...I would not leave you!''

''Yeah, right,'' he said, dragging his cast-free hand through his hair.

Megan got to her feet and went to stand directly in front of Ben.

''What are you trying to say, Ben?'' she said. ''That *you* wouldn't stand by me if *I* couldn't walk, or couldn't see? That you'd leave me?''

''Damn it, of course not, but this is different. I'm a man,'' he yelled, thumping himself on the chest. ''I have my pride, you know. I'm supposed to be big, strong, able to protect you, take care of you. How in the hell can I do that if I'm blind?''

"And what about *my* pride as a woman if I suddenly couldn't walk, or see? Tell me, Ben. Why are there different rules that pertain to you?"

"That's just the way it is, Megan!"

"And that's just a bunch of macho bull, Ben Rizzoli," she said, planting her hands on her hips. "And you're too intelligent to buy into it." She took a shuddering breath. "Do you want to know what I think? Don't answer that because I'm going to tell you anyway."

Unwelcome tears filled her eyes.

"I think," she said, her voice suddenly hushed, "that you don't really understand love, what it means, what it's capable of doing, how strong and fierce it can be."

She shook her head.

"I can't live like this anymore, Ben," she said, two tears spilling onto her pale cheeks. "I'm playing games, for heaven's sake, to enable me to be with you. That's not honest, and I hate it. It's also useless, because you see my love as something that will slip through your fingers like grains of sand when troubles disturb that sand.

"No, Ben, you just don't understand love—my love for you. My words, my being here with you, mean nothing. It's all in the now to you, just the now. That's not enough for me. I want a future, a forever, with you. Whether you can see, or not see. Walk, or not walk. Hear, or not hear. Talk, or not talk. *It doesn't matter, Ben, because I love you. But you...you just don't understand love.*"

"Megan—"

"I'm leaving, Ben."

"Megan, no, I—"

"You what? Want to marry me? Ask me to be your wife no matter what happens to your eyesight? Well?"

Ben opened his mouth, hesitated, then closed it again, shaking his head.

"I'll...I'll take what I need for tonight," Megan said, unable to stop the flow of tears streaming down her face and along her neck. "I'll come for the rest of my things when you're away at the office."

Megan ran across the room and up the stairs.

Ben turned to stare into the dwindling flames in the hearth.

When Megan returned carrying a small suitcase and wearing Andrea's borrowed jacket, she hesitated by the front door. "Goodbye, Ben," she said, her voice trembling.

As the click of the door being closed behind Megan reverberated through the air, Ben spun around.

"Megan?" he said.

But there was only silence in reply.

"Damn it."

He turned again to look into the hearth, only then realizing that his eyes were filled with tears.

Chapter Fourteen

You just don't understand love.

During the next three days and long, lonely nights, Megan's words pounded against Ben's mind.

Not understand love? The hell he didn't. He was putting Megan first, setting her free to have everything she deserved, and ignoring his own desire to keep her by his side.

You just don't understand love.

Ben sighed and sank onto a bench beneath an enormous tree on the town square. He was spending his lunch hour away from the office, having had enough of Sharon and Cynthia's sympathetic glances.

Hell, he thought, taking a bite of a fast-food hamburger, the whole town was probably buzzing, speculating as to why Megan Chastain had suddenly left Ben Rizzoli and moved into Hamilton House.

He knew that was where Megan was staying. Six of his patients had mentioned that fact, then waited eagerly to see if he would provide any grist for the gossip mill. His consistent comment was "Mmm."

Now what? he asked himself, taking a drink of soda. It was high noon on the fourth day since Megan had made her damnable accusation. Then left him. Tears streaming down her pale face. Sounding as though her heart was breaking.

Ben stared at the half-eaten hamburger in his hand, then shoved it into the paper sack, his appetite gone.

He'd hurt Megan, made her cry. He'd sworn he would never cause her pain, but he had, he truly had.

But he'd done the right thing.

You just don't understand love.

So, okay, suppose that maybe, just maybe, he didn't understand love. What wasn't he getting a grip on? What was causing him and Megan to be miles apart on the complicated subject?

Tired of chasing his own thoughts in circles, Ben got to his feet and walked to the opposite side of the tree where he tossed the sack in a trash container.

On the other side of the square beneath another huge tree he saw Professor Wilson sitting in his wheelchair reading a magazine.

An attractive woman, who appeared to be in her late forties, approached the professor with both hands behind her back.

With a smile she brought her hands forward, revealing two ice-cream cones. Professor Wilson took one of the cones, then slipped his hand to the nape of the woman's neck and pulled her close for a kiss.

Ben spun around and walked away, his mind racing.

An ice-cream cone, he thought. He hadn't been able to hear what Professor Wilson and his wife had said to each other, but what had transpired between them shouted their mutual love to the rooftops.

That woman had married Professor Wilson, knowing he was paralyzed. She'd pledged her love to the man, not caring that he couldn't walk, stand tall and strong beside her, protect her from harm. Who he was as a person had outweighed his infirmity.

Ben stopped and turned to look back at the professor and his wife. She had settled onto a bench next to the wheelchair. They were licking their cones and chatting, pointing upward occasionally as though they might be watching for glimpses of birds.

There is an aura of peacefulness about them, Ben thought, starting off again. Of rightness. Of love.

You just don't understand love.

Whether you can see, or not see. Walk, or not walk. Hear, or not hear. Talk, or not talk…it doesn't matter because I love you.

"Dr. Rizzoli!"

Ben stopped at the sudden sound of his name and saw a pretty, smiling young woman hurrying toward him.

"I'm so glad I saw you," she said when she reached him. "Brian and I just received the picture of our match, the baby that's been chosen for us by the Chinese officials in Beijing to be our daughter. We leave for China next week. Look, here she is.''

Ben stared at a picture of a solemn baby with hair sticking up in all directions and little fists tucked tightly beneath her chin.

''Congratulations, Janie,'' he said, smiling. ''She's a cutie.''

Janie laughed. ''No, she looks like an angry old man, but we think she's beautiful. We love her already, because she's ours in every sense of the word. I'm off to buy baby clothes. 'Bye.''

''Goodbye,'' Ben said quietly, resuming his walk.

That couple had been through hell, he mused. They'd undergone endless tests and countless attempts to have a child. It was finally determined that Brian had an unusual condition that hadn't been detected at first. For all practical purposes, Brian was sterile, and would never be able to give Janie a child.

But Janie still loved Brian. And now their dream was coming true in the form of that funny little kid from China, their daughter.

You just don't understand love.

Ben ran his fingertips over his now throbbing forehead, glanced at his watch, then headed for his vehicle.

It was time to get back to work. The afternoon would be busy, then he'd go home to what was once again just a house, a place to eat, sleep, stare into the fire in the hearth. A place filled with haunting memories of what had been, but no longer was.

Memories of Megan.

If he was blind, he would still, forever and always, be able to see her clearly in his mind as she nestled close to him on the sofa. He would still be able to savor her fresh-air-and-flowers aroma, hear her laughter, make sweet, sweet love to her through the hours of the night.

If he was blind, they would share, talk, care. He'd tell her how his lecture classes had gone that day. She'd relate the latest doing of her chickens, or whatever career she had chosen to pursue.

If he was blind, he could hold their adopted child in his arms, tell him stories, quiet his fears, be there for him as he grew up. He could tuck him in at night and assure his son that Daddy was there to keep the monsters beneath the bed at bay.

If he was blind, he would still be Ben Rizzoli.

And Megan Chastain would still love him, the person, the man.

This was the love that Megan had been struggling to get him to understand.

Ben slid behind the wheel of his vehicle, put the key in the ignition, but didn't turn it. He sat perfectly still, waiting for the voices in his mind to begin the barrage of reasons why Megan could not be his, why the future could not be theirs to share.

But there was only a peaceful silence, combined with a warmth that filled him, slowly, gently, touching his heart, mind, his very soul.

The war within him was over.

The battle was won.

He had conquered the anger, self-pity, the frustration and despair about his fate.

He *did* have a future that would be rich, and real, and fulfilling. He *did* have a purpose, a reason for being, something of value to offer as a teacher.

And now? Ben thought, starting the engine. Now he had to hope and pray that Megan would forgive him for the pain he'd caused her, would agree to be his wife, adopt a child with him, bring her sunshine into his world, not only in their now, but in their forever.

At six o'clock that night Ben entered the lobby of Hamilton House, carrying a small paper sack. He strode to the registration desk where Brandon was replacing the receiver to the telephone.

"It's about time you showed up, Rizzoli," Brandon said, glaring at Ben. "What took you so long?"

"I had some things I had to work through," Ben said quietly. "I just hope I'm not too late."

"Women's minds are beyond my comprehension," Brandon said. "All you can do is be honest and speak from your heart." He paused and narrowed his eyes. "I assume you've got your head on straight, and are ready to ask Megan to marry you?"

"That's the plan," Ben said, nodding. "But I'm a wreck. I blew it, Brandon, big time."

"Yep."

"Is Megan in her room?"

"Yep."

"She's been...well, really sad since she checked in here?"

"Yep."

"Damn it, Brandon, quit saying yep. What room is Megan in?"

"I can't tell you that," Brandon said. "It's against hotel policy to give out a guest's room number."

"Hamilton," Ben said, "I'll never be able to cut my own meat if I break my other hand punching you out, but that's exactly what's going to happen if you don't tell me where Megan is."

"She's in room four-twenty-two," Andrea said from behind Ben.

Ben spun around, nearly bumping into Andrea.

"Some rules have to be broken in the cause of true love," Andrea said, then kissed Ben on the cheek. "Go. Good luck."

"Ditto," Brandon said.

"Thanks," Ben muttered, then hurried toward the elevator.

Megan turned off the blow-dryer and heard some-one knocking on her door. She tightened the sash on the thigh-length, white terry-cloth robe she wore and hurried to answer the summons. She began speaking even as she was flinging open the door.

"I'm sorry. I couldn't hear over the—Ben!" Me-gan's eyes widened and her heart began to race. "Ben?"

"Hello, Megan," he said quietly.

There she was, Ben thought, the woman he loved with all his heart. She was beautiful.

Her hair was shiny, curling softly around her face, flushed a lovely pink from a recent shower. Those big, blue eyes were looking directly at him, making it difficult to breathe, to think straight.

This was it. What transpired in the next few minutes would determine his destiny. He would have a warm, sunshine future with Megan, or he would be alone in a world of cold darkness.

"May I come in?" he said.

"Oh. Well, yes. Yes, of course."

Megan stepped back to allow Ben to enter the room, closed the door, then leaned against it for support as she became acutely aware of the trembling of her legs.

Ben, her mind hummed. Her beloved Ben was there. Wearing dark slacks and a pale blue dress shirt open at the neck, he was magnificent. Oh, how she loved him, had missed him, had ached for the sight, and feel, and aroma of him.

Ben was there.

But why?

Ben turned in the center of the room and met Megan's gaze.

"I'd like to talk to you, Megan," he said. "Please. Could we sit down?"

"Yes."

Megan motioned toward an easy chair, then went to the edge of the bed, sinking onto it gratefully. Ben sat in the chair, rested his elbows on his knees and held the paper sack in both hands.

"You look..." they said in unison.

"Go ahead," Megan said.

"I was going to say that you look wonderful," Ben said.

"Oh, well, thank you." Megan smiled slightly. "I was going to say that you look terrible, exhausted."

"Yeah, well, I haven't been sleeping too great. I've had a lot on my mind. I've missed you, Megan."

"I've missed you, too, Ben," she said softly.

"I'm sorry I hurt you, caused you pain, made you cry," he said. "I swore I would never do that, but I sure as hell did." He took a shuddering breath and tightened his hold on the sack, despite the cumbersome cast. "I love you, Megan. Do you believe that?"

"Yes, I do, but—"

"I know. You couldn't live in just the now anymore, and I was convinced that was all I had to offer you. You said I didn't understand love."

"I didn't mean to be harsh, Ben."

"No, no, you were right. I didn't understand love, what it really meant, how powerful it was, how it was capable of coping with tremendous obstacles and adversities."

Megan nodded, then told herself to breathe as she felt a pain in her chest.

"I made the whole concept of love too complicated," Ben went on, his voice slightly raspy. "I mixed everything up together—my not being able to see someday, not being able to give you a child because of this menace hanging over me, everything I could never be for you.''

''Oh, Ben,'' Megan said, blinking away sudden tears.

''Love *is* complex,'' Ben said. ''But then again, it's not. It's very simple.'' He shook his head. ''Damn, I'm not making any sense.''

''Yes, yes, you are.''

''Megan, I think I probably fell in love with you the moment I found you in the woods. I loved you when you had no idea who you were, or what your personal circumstances were.

''I loved you when you got your memory back and you were so frightened about what Chastain was going to do.

''I loved you when I broke my hand decking that creep, and when you gathered your courage and stepped away from me so that you could close the door on your past while standing on your own two feet.

''Why did I love you despite all the changes you were going through, the events happening around you? Because you were still my Megan, the person, the woman. That's the simplistic beauty of the complexity of love.''

Megan nodded, then dashed two tears from her cheeks.

''When I'm blind, Megan,'' Ben said, his voice hoarse with emotion, ''I'll still be Ben Rizzoli, the person, the man you fell in love with. I'll teach the doctors of tomorrow. I'll hold the child we adopt in my arms and make certain he feels loved and safe. I'll make love with you as I've always done, reverently, lovingly. I'll still be Ben. Your Ben, if you'll have me.

"Megan, I'm asking you to forgive me for hurting you, for taking so long to understand love the way you do. I'm asking you to marry me, be my wife, for better, for worse, in sickness and in health, until death parts us in this world as we know it.

"Will...will you marry me?"

Megan flew off the bed and ran to where Ben sat. He dropped the sack and opened his arms just in time to catch her as she flung herself at him. He shifted her quickly across his lap, and she encircled his neck with her arms.

"Yes," she said, smiling through her tears. "Oh, yes, Ben Rizzoli, I'll marry you. I love you so very much."

"Thank God," he whispered. He closed his eyes for a long moment, then made no attempt to conceal the tears shimmering in his dark eyes when he looked at Megan again. "I love you, Megan, with all that I am, all that I'll be...forever."

Their lips met, tasting of salty tears. It was a kiss of forgiveness and commitment, of battles won and the sweet victory that was theirs. It was a kiss that spoke of a future together, dealing with all the joys and sorrows life would bring to them. It was a kiss of desire burning hotter with every beat of their racing hearts.

Ben broke the kiss to fumble with the sash on Megan's robe, then pushed aside the soft material to find her naked beneath. A groan rumbled deep in his chest.

He paid homage to one of her breasts as Megan flung her head back, eyes closed, as she savored the exquisite, sensuous sensations coursing through her. Ben moved to her other breast and she sighed in pure, feminine pleasure.

Ben raised his head. "I want you, Megan."

"Yes," she said, meeting his smoldering gaze. "I want you, too. So much."

She slipped off his lap and allowed the robe to fall to the floor. Ben stood and reached for the buckle on his belt.

"Ben?" Megan said. "That sack you brought in with you is getting soggy."

"Uh-oh." He snatched it from the floor and dropped it into the trash basket.

"What's in it?"

"An ice-cream cone," he said, smiling at her. "It was a symbol of the fact that I finally understand what love is all about. I'll explain it—" his glance slid over Megan's naked body in a heated path "—later."

Ben shed his clothes as quickly as the cast on his hand allowed, then they tumbled onto the bed.

They touched, kissed, explored anew all and everything about the one they loved, the person, the man, the woman, their partner for life.

When they could bear no more, Ben entered Megan's willing body, filling her, joining them to create one entity, one being. They soared to their place of ecstasy, bursting upon it as they called the name of the other, holding fast, knowing that in heart, mind and soul, they would never be parted again.

Afterward they lay close as Ben told Megan of his meeting with Professor Wilson, of later seeing the professor's wife bring her husband an ice-cream cone and the love that had emanated from the couple.

He related the story of the chance meeting with Janie, the woman who was so happy because she and her husband were about to become parents of a baby girl.

"It doesn't matter that Professor Wilson can't walk," Ben said. "It doesn't matter that Brian can never father a child. All that's important is the love those people have for each other. Thanks to you, Megan, I finally get it, finally understand. Man, I'm dense."

"Yep," Megan said, entwining her fingers in the moist curls on Ben's chest. "You're a stubborn Italian, Dr. Rizzoli."

"It won't be easy, Megan, all the things we'll have to deal with in the future."

"Nothing can defeat us, Ben. Not now. Not ever."

They were silent for several minutes, sated, contented, each lost in their own thoughts.

"Megan," Ben said finally, "I never called my brothers to get an update on the condition of their eyesight after all these months. I think I should do that now, while we're together."

"Yes, that's exactly what we should do. Your future is my future. My future is yours."

Ben chuckled. "Are we back to raising chickens?"

"No," Megan said, laughing. "I have a fabulous plan for what I want to do. I'll tell you all about it. But first…"

"First, we call my brothers. The days of playing ostrich are over. No more of that. No more anger, self-pity, the whole crummy nine yards. I'm just Ben, doing what I have to do."

"And I love you."

"Mmm."

"Mmm," Megan echoed.

An hour later Ben replaced the receiver to the telephone, then got to his feet and began to pace naked around the room.

"This is crazy," he said. "I don't know what to think. The brother who was having blurred vision had ordinary cataracts that have been tended to. He sees fine now. The next brother in line who was having daily headaches had a chronic sinus infection that has been treated. What in the hell does all this mean?"

Megan left the bed and went to Ben, wrapping her arms around his waist and looking up at him.

"It means," she said, "that no one, not your brothers, nor us, really knows what's going to happen. Maybe this mysterious menace has run its course, won't affect the rest of the Rizzoli males. Or maybe this is just a momentary reprieve, the lull before the storm that is yet to strike all of you. There's no way to know.

"But, Ben? However it goes, whatever happens, we'll be fine, because our love is stronger than anything that may attempt to defeat us. The now is ours. And, oh, my darling Ben, the future is ours, as well."

Ben kissed Megan deeply, then lifted her into his arms and carried her back to the bed.

No more words were spoken for a very long time. None were needed, because love had said it all.

Epilogue

Aunt Prudence and Aunt Charity bustled across the lobby of Hamilton House, chatting happily as they headed for the elevator.

"It was such a beautiful wedding," Aunt Prudence said with a wistful sigh. "Our Ben was so handsome, and our Megan was a beautiful bride. They're so very much in love, Charity."

"Most brides and grooms are, Pru," Charity said. "The big news is that Jennifer caught the bridal bouquet. Did you see the look on her face? You would have thought those flowers were rotten eggs."

"Jennifer doesn't wish to remarry, dear," Pru said.

"Oh, posh," Charity said as they entered the elevator. "What does *she* know?"

As the doors of the elevator swished closed, the front doors of the hotel opened once again. Andrea and Brandon strolled in, Brandon's arm encircling Andrea's shoulders as she dabbed at her nose with a tissue.

"I just adore weddings," Andrea said, sniffling.

Brandon chuckled. "Yep, you really look like you had fun. By the way, your nose is pink."

"I'm just so happy for Megan and Ben," Andrea said, then stopped walking and took a steadying breath. "There. I'm fine now. Crying tears of joy makes me hungry. Let's go into the dining room and have a snack."

Brandon bent over slightly and spoke to Andrea's stomach.

"Hello, hello, daughter of mine," he said. "What would you like to eat?"

"You're going to be eating crow if this baby is a boy," Andrea said.

"Would you care to make a small wager on our blessed event, my sweet?"

"Ah, a baby bet," a deep voice said. "That brings back fond memories."

Andrea and Brandon turned in the direction of the voice just as a man sitting in one of the high-back chairs in the lobby lowered a newspaper and smiled at them. He was tall, well-built, had dark, thick, auburn hair, brown eyes and ruggedly handsome features.

"I'll be damned," Brandon said, a grin breaking

across his face. "Jack MacAllister. How are you, Jack? Even more, what are you doing here?"

Jack MacAllister got to his feet, placed the newspaper in the chair, and strode forward to greet an approaching Brandon. The men shook hands, then punched each other on the shoulder.

"There's that strange male bonding number, or whatever it is," Andrea said, laughing. "The deeper the friendship, the harder you punch each other. Weird. Very weird."

"No worse than women who cry at weddings, then say they thoroughly enjoyed themselves," Brandon said. "Andrea, come meet this worthless bum."

Andrea joined the pair, Brandon made introductions, then Jack bowed.

"Jack MacAllister at your service, ma'am," he said. "It's a pleasure to meet the lovely lady who snagged Mr. Playboy of Manhattan here. I would have sworn it couldn't be done."

"Oh?" Andrea said, raising her eyebrows. "Do tell."

"No," Brandon said. "He's not telling any tales of the old days. Cork it, MacAllister. Let's go have a piece of pie and you can explain what you're doing so far from the Big Apple."

The trio was soon settled at a table in the hotel dining room, digging into slices of hot cherry pie.

"Delicious," Jack said, then paused. "So, when do you become a daddy, Brandon?"

"First of March," he said. "Thanksgiving is only

a couple of weeks away. Our baby girl will be here before we know it.''

"Easy for you to say," Andrea said. "You're not the one lugging her around." She rolled her eyes heavenward. "Now you've got me doing it. She could very well be a he."

"There was a time," Jack said, "when I would have said you needed my cousin, Forrest, to settle this squabble. Forrest won every baby bet that took place within our family, plus some extras on the side.

"My aunt Margaret, Forrest's mother, used to write or call me every time it happened. The man could not be beat. It was eerie, it really was."

"I remember Forrest," Brandon said. "Didn't he come to visit you in New York years ago? Sure, that was him. He came with his brothers, Ryan and Michael. None of them was married then."

"Yep, those were the boys, my cousins," Jack said. "Man, we sure had a good time going to all the—" he shot a quick glance at Andrea "—museums, didn't we?"

"Museums," Brandon said, nodding. "Yes. Lots of museums. Very informative, educational places, those museums."

"Oh, please, give it up," Andrea said, laughing.

"Not buying museums, huh?" Brandon said, smiling at her.

"Five bachelors on the loose in Manhattan?" she said. "Museums were the last thing on your swinging singles minds."

Jack shook his head. "Good thing there wasn't a

bachelor bet going on, or I'd be busted broke. I'm the only one of that rowdy group who isn't married. I would have put money on all of you guys being confirmed bachelors.''

"And my boyhood friend, Ben Rizzoli, got married today," Brandon said. "The odds are looking good, Jack. Maybe we should start a bachelor bet. I'll collect my money and buy you a wedding present."

"No way," Jack said, raising both hands. "I'm on my own and doing fine, thank you very much."

"Back up to this baby bet business," Andrea said. "You made it sound as though Forrest eventually lost his knack at winning."

"He did," Jack said, nodding. "He was on a roll, was really hot. He even predicted that his wife, Jillian, would have triplet girls and, son of a gun, she did. Those identical dolls are five and a half years old now.

"Anyway, let me tell you, it was getting pretty scary the way Forrest would nail the baby bet time after time."

"Then what happened?" Andrea said, leaning slightly forward.

"Well, there's this guy, Ted Sharpe. He's not a MacAllister, but he might as well be because he's like a member of the family. He's a cop, the partner of my cop cousin, Ryan.

"Ted said that his Hannah would have a baby girl on Christmas Day. Forrest predicted that she'd have a boy on New Year's Day. Remember now, Forrest was the baby bet champion of long standing.''

"And?'' Andrea said eagerly.

"Patricia Elizabeth, known as Patty, popped into the world to say hello to Santa Claus.''

"Forrest lost the baby bet?'' Andrea said.

"Yep,'' Jack said, nodding. "Not only that, but ever since then, the daddies have pegged it. As more little MacAllisters came along—and, man, there are a slew of them—the daddy-to-be has won the baby bet.''

"That's amazing,'' Andrea said, sinking back in her chair.

"I love it.'' Brandon ran his hand down his tie and puffed out his chest. "The daddies are geniuses. We, sweet wife, are having a girl.''

Andrea stared at Brandon with wide eyes. "I'm beginning to believe you.''

"You should,'' Jack said. "Brandon and I have been friends for many years. That makes him a MacAllister of sorts. Yes, ma'am, I'd put my money on a girl in a baby bet based on Brandon's prediction.''

Andrea laughed. "You're as cocky as Brandon is, Jack. I like the idea of a bachelor bet much better.''

"I'm outta here,'' Jack said, pretending to rise from his chair.

"You haven't told me why you're here in Prescott yet,'' Brandon said.

"As unbelievable as it may sound,'' Jack said, "I

dropped out of the fast lane of New York, just as you did, Brandon.''

"You're kidding," Brandon said.

"I told you it was unbelievable. I woke up one morning in my apartment in Manhattan and walked smack into a wall, because I thought I was still in a hotel in Hong Kong. Enough was enough.''

"What type of work do you do?" Andrea said.

"I'm an architect," Jack said. "I think there's an extra gene or something that some MacAllisters get. There are a bunch of architects in our family.

"There's going to be a reunion of the whole clan at Christmastime over in Ventura, California. I folded my tent in New York and started driving cross-country a month ago, stopping, exploring, when the mood hit. I decided to look you up, Brandon, since I was in the neighborhood.

"When I eventually get to California in time for the holidays, I'm going to join the firm of Mac-Allister Architects, Incorporated.''

"I'll be damned," Brandon said. "Oops—mustn't swear in front of my daughter. So, you're in no rush to leave Prescott?''

Jack shrugged and took another bite of pie.

Andrea and Brandon looked at each other, then Andrea nodded.

"It's fate," she said. "Meant to be.''

"Hmm?" Jack said, looking up again.

"We've decided to have an architect draw up plans for our house, because we just haven't been able to find what we're looking for,'' Brandon said. "What do you say, buddy? Want the job?''

"On one condition,'' Jack said, narrowing his eyes as he looked at Andrea.

"Which is?'' she said.

"That you forget all about this bachelor bet nonsense,'' Jack said.

Andrea Cunningham Hamilton just smiled.

* * * * *

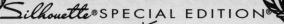

Silhouette®SPECIAL EDITION®

That SPECIAL Woman!

She's a wife, mother—she's you! And beside each Special Edition woman stands a wonderfully special man! Don't miss these upcoming titles only from Silhouette Special Edition!

♥♥♥

May 1999 HER VERY OWN FAMILY
by Gina Wilkins (SE #1243)
Family Found: Sons & Daughters

All her life, Brynn Larkin had yearned for a home—and a wonderful husband. So when sexy surgeon Joe D'Allesandro offered Brynn a helping hand—and made her an honorary member of his loving clan—had she finally found her very own family?

♥♥♥

July 1999 HUNTER'S WOMAN
by Lindsay McKenna (SE #1255)
Morgan's Mercenaries: The Hunters

Catt Alborak was ready for battle when she was thrown back together with Ty Hunter, the mesmerizing mercenary from her past. As much as the headstrong lady doc tried to resist her fierce protector, their fiery passion knew no bounds!

♥♥♥

September 1999 THEIR OTHER MOTHER
by Janis Reams Hudson (SE #1267)
Wilders of Wyatt County

Sparks flew when widowed rancher Ace Wilder reluctantly let Belinda Randall care for his three sons. Would the smitten duo surrender to their undeniable attraction—and embark on a blissful future together?

Look for That Special Woman! every other month from some of your favorite authors!
Available at your favorite retail outlet.

Silhouette®

If you enjoyed what you just read,
then we've got an offer you can't resist!

Take 2 bestselling love stories FREE!

Plus get a FREE surprise gift!

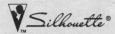

Sometimes families are made in the most unexpected ways!

Don't miss this heartwarming new series from
Silhouette Special Edition®, Silhouette Romance®
and popular author

DIANA WHITNEY

Every time matchmaking lawyer
Clementine Allister St. Ives brings a couple
together, it's for the children...
and sure to bring romance!

August 1999
I NOW PRONOUNCE YOU MOM & DAD
Silhouette Special Edition #1261
Ex-lovers Powell Greer and Lydia Farnsworth knew *nothing*
about babies, but Clementine said they needed to learn—fast!

September 1999
A DAD OF HIS OWN
Silhouette Romance #1392
When Clementine helped little Bobby find his father, Nick Purcell
appeared on the doorstep. Trouble was, Nick wasn't Bobby's dad!

October 1999
THE FATHERHOOD FACTOR
Silhouette Special Edition #1276
Deirdre O'Connor's temporary assignment from Clementine
involved her handsome new neighbor, Ethan Devlin—and
adorable twin toddlers!

Available at your favorite retail outlet.

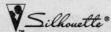

"Fascinating—you'll want to take
this home!"
—**Marie Ferrarella**

"Each page is filled with a brand-new
surprise."
—**Suzanne Brockmann**

"Makes reading a new and joyous
experience all over again."
—**Tara Taylor Quinn**

See what all your favorite authors
are talking about.

Coming October 1999 to a retail store near you.

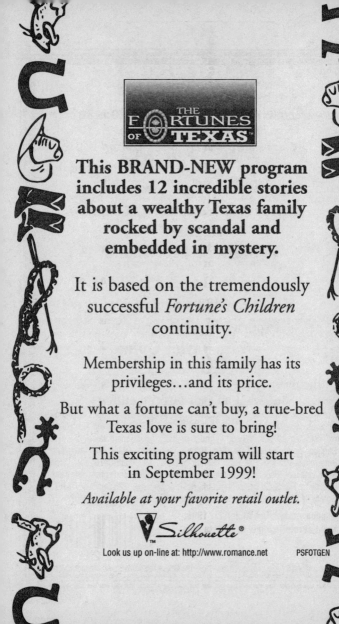

THE FORTUNES OF TEXAS

Membership in this family has its privileges...and its price.
But what a fortune can't buy,
a true-bred Texas love is sure to bring!

Silhouette® brings you a **BRAND-NEW** program that includes 12 incredible stories about a wealthy Texas family rocked by scandal and embedded in mystery. It is based on the tremendously popular **Fortune's Children** continuity.

Watch for the first book in September 1999 at your favorite retail outlet.

MILLION DOLLAR MARRIAGE
by **Maggie Shayne**

Use this coupon on any Fortunes of Texas title and receive $1 off.

THE FORTUNES OF TEXAS™

Membership in this family has its privileges...and its price.
But what a fortune can't buy,
a true-bred Texas love is sure to bring!

Silhouette® brings you a **BRAND-NEW** program that includes 12 incredible stories about a wealthy Texas family rocked by scandal and embedded in mystery. It is based on the tremendously popular Fortune's Children continuity.

Watch for the first book in September 1999 at your favorite retail outlet.

MILLION DOLLAR MARRIAGE
by Maggie Shayne

Use this coupon on any Fortunes of Texas title and receive $1 off.

$1.00 OFF!
the purchase of any **Fortunes of Texas** title

RETAILER: Harlequin Enterprises Ltd. will pay the face value of this coupon plus 8¢ if submitted by customer for this specified product only. Any other use constitutes fraud. Coupon is nonassignable, void if taxed, prohibited or restricted by law. Consumer must pay any government taxes. Valid in U.S. only. Nielson Clearing House customers—Mail to: Harlequin Enterprises Limited, P.O. Box 880478, El Paso, TX 88588-0478, U.S.A. Non NCH retailer—For reimbursement submit coupons and proof of sales directly to: Harlequin Enterprises Ltd., Retail Sales Dept., 225 Duncan Mill Rd., Don Mills (Toronto), Ontario M3B 3K9, Canada.

Coupon expires December 31, 1999. Valid at retail outlets in U.S. only.

Silhouette®

5 65373 00076 2   (8100) 1 07062

PSFOTUS